The Painter

RICK LOVEDAY

The characters and events in this book are fictitious. Any similarity to actual events or persons, living or dead, is purely coincidental and not intended by the author.

Cover design by Rick Loveday
Cover painting by Kathy Cord

ISBN: 978-0-6151-6748-0
Printed in the United States of America.

First Printing: November 2006
10 9 8 7 6 5 4 3 2 1

This book is dedicated to my parents, Richard and Mary, for their love, support, and encouragement. Without them, this book would not have been possible.

Chapter One

The shimmering sun broke through the calm Atlantic Ocean and began its daily arc through the sky, bringing with it all the makings of a beautiful, crisp mid-September morning outside of the tiny seaside town of Edisto Beach, South Carolina. Sitting in the studio at my house, barely a hundred yards from the water, I felt the gentle morning breeze as it trickled through the open window. I marveled in wonder at the view as the beauty of the early morning sunrise soaked into my very being. The water was forever a part of me. The cool, salty Atlantic flowed through my veins. The smell alone instantly invigorated me.

The crashing waves pounded against the shore and snapped me out of my daze. I stared out of the window, scanning the waterfront as the white-crested waves broke over the beach and left a trail of bubbly foam on the sand. In a small pool of water just above the shoreline stood a family of sandpipers digging for their morning meal of crustaceans. Further up the shoreline, I spotted a lone blue heron perched regally on a large piece of beached driftwood.

My lips curved upward into a smile as I reached for a paint brush. The soft bristles soaked up the watercolors and the canvas quickly exploded with life and color. Cool blue waves hung, frozen in time, above the gleaming white sand. The rising sun cast a golden reflection over the water's rippling surface. Majestic oranges, brilliant reds, every vibrant color was forever captured on the canvas.

With the scenery in place, I went on to add the finer details that always gave so much life to my paintings. Soft touches such as seaweed and driftwood in the sand or trails of footprints gave the piece a natural, livable feel. I soon began to brush in the body of the great blue heron.

"It's really beautiful, isn't it?" came a voice from the doorway in a mere whisper.

I spun around on the stool to find my wife leaning against the door frame. Her sandy blonde hair fought to escape from a disheveled ponytail. Small, barely visible, crow's feet were etched in the corners of her eyes. Her lips curved upward in a perpetual smile. Her skin was a little pale, but still smooth as silk to the touch. To me, she remained as beautiful today as the day we married.

"Did I wake you up?" I asked. "I tried to be as quiet as possible because you were sleeping so soundly."

"No, you didn't." She moved behind me and draped her arms over my shoulders. Her warm lips pressed against my temple. "I woke up a couple of minutes ago. You were already out of bed, so I knew you would be in here painting."

I struggled to think as her intoxicating scent washed over me. "Where else would I be? This is one of the best views in the entire house. Well, except for you, of course."

Pale red circles expanded from the center of Rebecca's

cheeks. She nodded toward the open window. "I love watching the sun rise, feeling its warmth on my face. It makes me forget about everything else in the world."

"How does your back feel this morning?"

Her hand drifted down to the small of her back. "It still hurts. I don't know what I did to it. All I can think of is that I must have pulled something a while ago, maybe when we did the inventory at the shop."

"I'll give you a massage later on, if you think that'll help."

Rebecca nodded at me and smiled. I reciprocated her smile as she walked toward the window and stared in silence at the morning seascape. The rhythmic crash of the waves against the shoreline filtered in through the window. The water's calmness and strength flowed through my body. All the sounds faded into nothing as I watched her stare out the window. The beauty before me was far greater than anything I could ever see outside.

"There's something I want you to do for me," she said, finally breaking the silence.

"Anything you want."

"I want you to paint a portrait of me." She grew silent for a moment as she turned from the window to face me. "I realized that the last portrait you did of me was over ten years ago. I just thought it was time for an updated one."

"Of course, all you ever had to do was ask and I would have done a new portrait for you anytime."

She turned back toward the window. I pushed myself up from the easel and wrapped my arms around her waist, taking both of her hands. Her body melted into mine as I pulled her into me and kissed her cheek. My chin rested on her shoulder and we both stared out of the window at the water.

"I love you," I whispered into her ear and the hairs on her neck stood on end.

She turned around and draped her arms around my neck. A flirtatious smirk spread across her face. "I know." She rose up on her tiptoes and pressed her lips to mine. "I'm going to make some coffee. Do you want some?"

I nodded and then added, "I'll start your portrait later today, if you feel up to posing for me." She smiled then disappeared into the hallway.

After she left, I turned back toward the window and leaned against the wooden frame. The family of sandpipers still pecked through the sand on the shoreline. Two of the smaller birds scampered through the puddles in a lively game of tag. The driftwood further up the shore where the heron once perched now stood empty. Apparently, I would have to finish the rest of the heron from memory. I returned to the easel and sat down, reaching for a brush to continue painting. My eyes closed and the image of the heron splashed against my eyelids. I studied its magnificent body in my mind's eye for a moment before my hand rose toward the canvas.

"We're out of coffee," Rebecca called to me from the kitchen.

"Do you want me to run to the store and get some?"

"Do you mind?"

"No, not at all. Just give me a minute to finish up in here."

The rest of the great blue heron's elegant body appeared on the canvas in a matter of a few minutes. After cleaning the brush in a cup of water and setting it on the table, I backed away from the easel and walked toward the kitchen.

I stopped in the doorway and grabbed the keys from the hook next to the phone. Rebecca sat at the kitchen table, staring blankly out of the window. I moved behind her then leaned down to hug her. "I'll be back soon."

I pressed my lips to her cool cheek, breathing in her fragrance again, then walked out of the room toward the front door. Rebecca got up from the table and followed me out, stopping on the porch as I continued on to the car. She waved as I backed down the driveway then stepped back inside the house as I pulled away.

*   *   *

Every time I drove through Edisto Beach, I was reminded that it was a tiny beachfront town nothing at all like the area of Wilmington where I grew up. But the rural nature and small community aspect was one of the main attractions of the town, at least for me. Just a single, two-lane road connected the whole of Edisto Island with the thoroughfares that ran from Charleston to Savannah.

Even though it was out of the way, I always made it a point to pass through the heart of Edisto Beach: the docks. The smell of fish permeated the air through the closed car windows. Next to the small buildings, stacked crab pots reached up to the height of the roof and the empty fish boxes sat in piles beside them. The area was the textbook definition of a true fishing community. The laid-back calmness of the area felt just as strong as the first time I visited the town with Rebecca and her family all those many years ago. It had been love at first sight.

The trip to the store and back took less than twenty minutes. The next thing I knew, I was pulling back into my driveway. The relaxation of the short drive faded in an instant the moment I stepped into the house. The darkened rooms screamed with an unnerving silence and lack of activity. My mind raced as I stepped into the kitchen. I set the coffee can down on the counter and looked around, wondering where my wife was.

"Rebecca?" I called out. "Honey, I'm back. Bec?"

The deafening silence washed over me as I eased out of the kitchen and down the hall toward the bedroom and studio. At once, my fears subsided when I found Rebecca curled up on the couch in my studio, asleep. I scolded myself for worrying so much about nothing and, not wanting to disturb her, turned to leave the room. I paused in the doorway for a brief moment. My gaze drifted around the room, from Rebecca, to the easel, to one of my many sketchbooks. I tiptoed across the room, grabbing a pencil and one of the books from the table, and then sat down in a chair across from her. With quick, fluid strokes, I sketched Rebecca sleeping on the couch, recreating the exact scene before me. The way her arm curled back under the pillow to support her head, the peaceful and contented smile on her lips, the few strands of hair falling across her cheek, not a single detail missed.

After completing the initial sketch, I continued with another, then one more, until nearly forty-five minutes had passed. I remained completely oblivious to everything else until Rebecca groaned and stirred in her sleep.

Her eyes fluttered open and darted from side to side. "What are you doing?" she asked as she sat up and stretched.

"I'm just sketching you. I got back from the store and found you asleep in here."

"What time is it?"

"It's almost ten."

"I didn't mean to fall asleep," she grumbled. "It was just so peaceful and relaxing sitting by the window."

"You don't have to tell me that," I replied, smiling. "I didn't have the heart to wake you up."

"Aw, you should have."

"Well, you looked so peaceful. Plus, I ended up drawing a few sketches of you."

"I must look horrible."

"That's definitely not possible."

Rebecca tilted her head and raised an eyebrow at me. A small grin slipped through her pressed lips. "Well, can I see them? Can I?" She begged like a child on Christmas.

I sat down next to Rebecca and handed her the sketches. She studied each one in complete silence, pausing only to shake her head and grin sheepishly at me.

"So what do you think?" I asked.

Without a word, Rebecca placed the sketches down on the table and turned to face me. A radiant smile came to her face and she hooked her arms around my neck and latched on to me.

"I take it you like them," I said with a wink and leaned in to kiss her. When I began to pull away, she grabbed the back of my head and pulled me back in. Her lips pressed firmly against mine. When she finally released me, I found it a struggle to breathe. The best I could manage was a huge, dumbfounded grin as I blinked my eyes in a failed attempt to regain my composure.

"I'm going to go make that coffee now."

Rebecca sauntered out of the room, toward the kitchen. I tried to stand up, but my knees buckled and I collapsed back on the couch. My lips quivered and my heart skipped several beats. The warmth of her mouth still resonated on my lips. It took several minutes before I managed to push myself up from the couch and, aided by the table, walk to the easel. The blank canvas glared back at me, begging to be covered. I struggled to break the mesmerizing trance it had over me and glanced out of the window.

The crash of metal clanging against the floor echoed through the house. "Bec? Is everything all right?"

It took only a matter of seconds for me to reach the kitchen. I found Rebecca on her hands and knees in the middle of the floor, brushing the spilled coffee grounds into a pile with her hand. I knelt down next to her. "What happened?"

"Nothing, I just went all clumsy for a second and dropped the coffee. I can't believe I did that."

"Oh, don't worry about it. It's no big deal." I reached over and tucked a few loose strands of hair behind her ear. The back of my hand brushed against her cheek. "Why don't you go relax while I clean this up? You take it easy so you'll be up for posing later."

"Are you sure?"

"I'm sure. I'll bring the coffee back to you when it's ready."

Rebecca pulled herself to her feet and smiled down at me. I returned her smile and winked before I started to clean up the spilled coffee grounds. She turned and walked out of the room. As she left, it looked like she was clutching her side. I sat there on my knees, staring at the empty doorway. It had been her back that was sore, not her side. I shrugged it off and made a mental note to give her the massage I had promised to see if that would help with the soreness.

When I returned to the studio with the coffee, Rebecca sat on the couch, once again staring out of the window at the water. I set the coffee on the table and sat down next to her. I looped my arm around her shoulder and gave a gentle squeeze.

"Are you sure you're okay?"

"Yes, I'm fine," she answered without taking her eyes off of the water. Then, as if feeling my eyes locked onto her, she looked over at me and offered a weak smile. "I'm fine, really. I guess I'm just feeling a bit restless with taking off from work the past week. I just don't like having nothing to do."

"I know the feeling. Oh, here's your coffee," I retrieved one of the cups from the table and handed it to her. The fragrant hazelnut aroma filled the room. "Careful, it's hot."

"Thank you." She breathed in the scent then took a sip. "When do you think you'll be able to start on my portrait?"

"Are you sure that you're up to it with your back and all?"

Rebecca nodded.

"I can start sketching it now to get an idea of what pose you want…if you'd like." I set my mug on the table and grabbed the sketchbook. "How do you want it to look? What kind of pose?"

"I want the sun shining down on me through the window."

I grabbed a chair and sat down across from her. Rebecca squirmed about on the couch as she readied her pose. After flipping through the sketchbook to the first blank page, I glanced over at her and began drawing. It took just a few minutes to finish the first sketch.

"This is perfect," she replied, staring at the paper in her hands. "I love how the light shines down on my face. The subtle shadows make it so beautiful."

I reached for the cup from the table and took a quick sip.

"How long do you think it will take?"

"I'll need to sketch it out on the canvas first. But once I start painting, no more than a day or so, depending on how long you can sit for me."

"Good." Rebecca smiled at me then angled back toward the

window and stared out over the water. The sound of her breathing was the only noise in the room for the longest time before she turned back to me. "I'm going to fix something to eat while you get things set up in here. Do you want anything?"

"Yes, that would be great. Thank you."

Rebecca leaned over and kissed my cheek before standing up and heading for the hall. After she left, I sat down at the easel and began setting up the canvas and paints. I found a charcoal pencil after a quick search through my tackle box and started to sketch the basic outline onto the canvas. Rebecca soon returned with a tray of food and two drinks. She set the tray on the table and sat down on the couch, patting the cushion next to her.

"Here you go." She handed me one of the plates.

A thought pushed its way to the forefront of my mind. I stopped eating and looked over at Rebecca. "Who's covering at the shop today? Leslie again?"

"Yeah...again. I had been thinking about giving her more responsibilities to go along with the Assistant Manager title. So I guess it all works out."

"I'm glad it's going so well. She's a terrific girl."

"Yes, she is, isn't she?"

The corners of Rebecca's lips curled up just a little at the mention of Leslie's name. I thought of all the help Leslie had been with the extra hours and solo days the past couple of weeks. If it hadn't been for Leslie's help, Rebecca would have probably had to close up the shop temporarily until her back stopped bothering her. Leslie definitely deserved the promotion.

* * *

As soon as we finish eating, Rebecca grabbed my empty

plate, piled it on the tray with hers, and disappeared into the hall. She returned a little while later wearing a long, flowing white dress that dangled temptingly off of her shoulders. The silky fabric clung to every sultry curve of her body and stopped just above her ankles. My heart skipped a beat as our eyes locked. Her bare feet scuffed against the carpet as she crossed the room toward me.

Rebecca stopped in front of me and ran her hands along the dress to straighten out the nonexistent wrinkles. "Do you like it?" All I could manage was a nod. She eased down on the couch and tucked her legs under her. They disappeared beneath the rippling waves of silk and the folds of her dress.

I grabbed the charcoal pencil and drew a rough sketch of Rebecca, the couch and the window. A few minutes later, I dropped the pencil on the table and spun the easel around to face her. She leaned forward from her pose and smiled at the sketch.

"Martin, it's perfect. I love it."

I spun the easel back toward me and retrieved the palette from the table. A soft squeeze from the tube of Cadmium Yellow along with a small dab of Titanium White spiraled together as I mixed the acrylic paint to form the pale yellow color of the walls of the studio. I grabbed a wide brush and cut it through the mixed paint, allowing the soft bristles to soak up the color. Long, horizontal strokes of the brush over the taut, rough canvas left a trail of color as I filled in the entire background area.

With a few strokes of Burnt Umber, I brushed the wood window frame into the background over the yellow wall. I squeeze a few drops of Emerald Green on the palette to use for the couch. My plan was to do the quick basics for the background and add the finer details later on via layering. Right now my only concern was getting as much of the painting on canvas as I could while Rebecca was sitting in front of me.

The remaining Burnt Umber mixed with some more Titanium White and the smallest drop of Cadmium Red produced the perfect skin tone. I brushed in the area where Rebecca's face would be, continuing down to fill in her neckline before painting in her arms.

Titanium White with a dab of Titan Buff mixed together to solve the biggest challenge of matching the creamy, white silk color of her dress. The brush glided over the canvas and pulled the subtle figure under her dress out from the background.

The painting came alive with vibrant colors, reflecting the scene that I saw sitting on the couch in front of me. I began going back over the ambiguous shapes and added more tone and color and depth, which brought out the refined details. Time flew by as the painting became more and more alive.

"Are you okay?"

"I'm fine," Rebecca responded, yawning. "How long has it been?"

"A couple of hours, so far. Are you getting tired?"

"Not really," she admitted. "It's just the sitting in one spot, not being able to move. It's starting to make my back hurt."

"Tell you what, go lie down. We can finish this up tomorrow, if you're up to it."

Rebecca smiled and, with a slight nod at me, stood up and walked toward the bedroom. I remained sitting in front of the canvas, staring at the half-finished painting. Rebecca's piercing blue eyes gazed back at me out of the blurry canvas.

Chapter Two

After cleaning the brushes and straightening up the studio, I meandered toward the kitchen and browsed through the pantry. The well-stocked shelves offered no help in deciding what to fix for dinner. I closed the doors and my gaze drifted up to the clock on the wall above the doorway. Rebecca was sitting on the bed, leaning up against the wall, engrossed in a book when I popped my head through the bedroom door.

"Hey, I just realized it's only four."

"I thought it was later than that," Rebecca replied, setting her book down.

"Yeah, so did I. I was thinking about taking a walk down the beach before fixing dinner. You want to join me, or is your back too sore?"

"Sure, I'd love to. Just give me a minute."

Rebecca grabbed a jacket and, moments later, we strolled hand in hand down the beach as we had done countless times before. The pounding surf bubbled and foamed over the packed sand a few feet from our path. Three seagulls skimmed just above the water in search of food. We walked down the shoreline quietly talking and laughing. It felt like only a few minutes had passed, but when I glanced down at my watch I was shocked to realize that nearly thirty minutes had gone by. We stopped walking and I turned to face Rebecca, taking her other hand in mine. I leaned closer and kissed her then wrapped my arms around her in a tender embrace. I didn't notice the strained look on her face until I pulled back. During the walk, I had been so focused on the moment that I hadn't picked up on the change in her demeanor.

"Are you okay?"

"Yeah, I'm fine. Just a little tired suddenly."

"Do you need to sit down for a minute?"

"No, I'll be fine. Let's just head back now."

"As you wish," I responded, smiling. "I need to start dinner soon anyway."

I held out my arm and Rebecca took the hint and wrapped both of her arms around mine. She rested her head on my shoulder. We began the familiar trek back to the house, huddled closely together.

* * *

Neither of us had been all that hungry when we got back to the house so we decided to put off dinner until later. Rebecca retreated back to the bedroom while I ventured into the living room and collapsed onto the faded brown sofa. My eyes rested on the television for a brief second as I contemplated turning it on. Painting and spending time with Rebecca usually took up the majority of my time, but I tried to catch a couple of the news programs in the evenings. I reached for the remote on the coffee table, but paused. Next to the remote was a copy of the *Tao Te Ching*, by Lao Tzu, that Rebecca had bought for me a few months earlier. I left the remote where it was and grabbed the book instead, deciding to knock out one of the four to six books I tried to read each month.

From the first page, its passages drew me in so much that I was completely oblivious to everything surrounding me.

"Hello? Anyone home?"

I put the book on the table and walked toward the door. Leslie closed the front door behind her just as I stepped into the foyer.

"Hey, Martin," she greeted me with a wide smile.

"Leslie? This is a surprise. I didn't know you were stopping by tonight."

As Leslie took her jacket off and hung it by the door, I paused for a moment. Though I'd known her since the day she was born—I had been best friends with her father, Paul Taylor, since high school—I stopped to admire the person she had grown into.

A beautiful woman of twenty-two, Leslie had graduated from the University of North Carolina with a degree in History. After graduation, she followed her heart, otherwise known as her boyfriend of three years, to historic Charleston, South Carolina, thinking the relationship would lead to marriage. Two months after moving, the jerk abruptly broke up with her in order to go 'find himself.' He left Leslie alone in a new place where she hardly knew anyone. She made a call to Rebecca and me and told us what had happened. A week later, we helped her find a place to live and got her a job at Rebecca's shop. That was almost a year ago. In that year, both Rebecca and I began to see Leslie as the daughter we never had.

"So?"

"Oh, did you say something?" I asked, snapping out of my

daze.

"Yeah, I was asking how Rebecca was feeling," she responded, grinning from ear to ear. "But I'm thinking that I should be asking about you instead."

"Aren't you just the comedian." I motioned for her to follow me into the living room. "She's doing okay. Her back is still really sore, though."

"Well, I hope she feels better soon. It's not the same at the shop without her."

"I'm sure she will be back before you know it. We couldn't keep her away from that place if we tried," I assured her. "So how's your dad doing?"

"He's doing well. Getting ready to start two new development projects in Charleston and Beaufort."

"Sounds like his company is taking off."

"Yeah, it looks that way. It's been kind of rough for him since leaving his old job, but it's all worth it now." She reached into her bag and pulled out a folder. "I brought by the sales reports for the week to go over with her. Do you think she's up for company?"

"She's back in the bedroom reading. You can go and check with her if you'd like."

"Thanks," Leslie replied as she walked back toward the bedroom. She stopped before rounding the corner. "Oh, by the way, you've had a great week. Three of your paintings sold in the past two days."

"Hey, that's great! Thanks for letting me know."

Leslie smiled at me before heading back to the bedroom. I could feel the warmth spreading through my cheeks as I sat back down on the couch and picked up my book. The attempt to continue reading ended in complete failure. All I could think about was the three paintings that sold. I knew it shouldn't be much of a surprise because I usually sold around five to six paintings a week, but I still felt overwhelmed when a piece sold. Even after all these years, I guess it still surprised me that people would want to have my work hanging in their home.

After twenty unfruitful minutes, I completely gave up trying to read. I left the book on the coffee table and began to wander. The next thing I knew I was standing on the porch leaning against the railing. As I stared out over the black water, my eyes fell shut. The prevailing sound of the gentle waves crashing against the unseen shore rang in my ears. The front door opened and Leslie stepped onto the porch then leaned against the railing next to me. The evening breeze whipped through her hair that had escaped from her ponytail. She reached up to tuck the wayward strands behind her ear.

"It's amazing, isn't it? So much power, but still the gentleness of the water."

"There's nothing like it in the world."

"I'm kind of jealous of you two. Well, mainly just of the house. I would love to be able to afford a place on the water like this."

"We could never afford this place now. We just got lucky that the land was dirt cheap twenty years ago when we moved down here. There was only the one road on the island and it was over an hour's drive to anything. But the selling point was the beauty here."

"I bet the cheap price didn't hurt, either."

A small chuckle escaped from my throat. "No, that definitely didn't hurt."

"Well, I'm going to head back home. I'll try to stop by in a few days to go over more of the paperwork."

"That would be nice. Maybe you could come for dinner, too?"

"I'd love that. I'll give you a call and let you know."

She scampered down the steps and, through the darkness, made her way to her car. Her blinding headlights lit up the porch, doubling the number of stars I saw in the clear black void of night. I waved at her as she pulled away from the house. The two red dots of her tail lights disappeared and my attention quickly refocused on the water.

*   *   *

The radiant full moon cast a white glow overhead in the night sky. I led a blindfolded Rebecca down the steps and along a tiny, lantern-lit path on the beach toward a small table. The faint flames of two burning candles flickered in the gentle evening breeze. I pulled out one of the chairs and helped Rebecca sit down. After kissing her on the cheek, my hand drifted back to the blindfold and I slipped it off, revealing the surprise. I had spent the better part of the evening preparing the romantic dinner for two on the beach barely a few feet from the ocean and under a full moon. Her eyes welled up with tears as she smiled at me when I sat down across from her.

"What are you thinking?" I whispered.

Rebecca sat silent for a second and just stared at me. "I can't believe you did all of this for me. It's just so unbelievable."

"Well, you deserve only the best. Now let's eat, before it gets cold."

Rebecca removed the cover from the plate in front of her. On her plate was a helping of linguini with sautéed shrimp in a garlic butter sauce along with a side of steamed vegetables. She leaned forward and breathed in the fragrant aroma of the meal.

"You always find some way to blow my mind."

"It's my job. And you know that I take pride in my work."

Rebecca twirled a few strands of linguini then speared a shrimp and raised the fork to her mouth. Her eyes shut as her lips closed over the tightly wound cocoon. "This is the most succulent shrimp I've ever tasted. How did you make it?"

"I'll never tell. My culinary secrets will go with me to my grave."

A dark shadow passed over Rebecca's face. Her eyes dropped and she stared at the table. I slid out of my chair and knelt down in the sand, slipping my arm around her and resting my head on her lap.

"I'm sorry. I shouldn't have said that. I wasn't thinking."

"No, it's not that. It's just..."

Rebecca trailed off and turned away from me. She sat there in complete silence, just staring at the crashing waves. I followed her gaze over the water before taking her hand. Rebecca's attention drifted back to me as I pulled her out of the chair and led her a few steps out onto the sand.

"Let's try not to think about it now. Not tonight."

"I'll give it a shot."

Pulling Rebecca close to me, my lips brushed against hers and I held her as we rocked back and forth on the beach. The evening waves crashed into the shoreline as the two of us danced to music that could only be heard in our heads.

* * *

My eyes snapped open from the same recurring dream that had been plaguing my nights several times a week for the past few months. It first started when Rebecca told me about the dream she had been having. There must have been something about the closeness of our relationship that linked us together because not long after she told me about her dream of our candlelit dinner on the beach, I began to have the exact same dream. And if that wasn't weird enough, on the nights she would have the dream I did as well.

I rolled over to ask Rebecca if she had just had the dream, but when I faced her direction the bed was empty. My gaze drifted around the room. The bathroom door was closed, but there was no light escaping from beneath it. I climbed out of bed and wandered through the darkness out of the bedroom. Once in the hall, I stopped outside the open door of the studio.

Pausing in the doorway, I spied Rebecca sitting on the stool in front of the half-finished portrait. She clutched the afghan that usually rested on the back of the couch around her shoulders. I watched as she picked up one of the paint tubes and unscrewed the lid. She took a whiff of the commonplace aroma of paint that permeated our house. She set the paint back on the table and ran her fingers across the unpainted area of the canvas. A single tear escaped from her eye and carved its path down her cheek, leaving a moist trail glinting in the moonlight. Pausing on her jaw, the lone tear released and fell toward the table, landing in the still open tube of paint. Several more tears rolled down her cheeks and fell in the paint and onto the table. I stepped forward out of the shadows of the hall.

"Bec?"

Rebecca spun around toward the doorway. "Martin? How long have you been there?"

"Only a few seconds." I walked across the room and knelt down next to her. "I woke up and you were gone." My lips pressed together and I took a moment to rub her shoulders. "What's wrong?"

"I just couldn't sleep."

My arm slipped around her shoulder. "Did you have the dream again?"

Rebecca's eyes glistened in the dim light. "How did you know?"

"I had it, so I figured there was a good chance you did, too."

"I did, but it's nothing."

"Honey, you're sitting here in the middle of the night, crying. Don't tell me that nothing's wrong."

Rebecca looked deep into my eyes. The moonlight filtering in through the window provided just enough light for me to see my reflection in her eyes. "It's just that...I...," she trailed off and glanced away, refusing to hold eye contact. I reached up and caressed her shoulder before turning her to face me again. "I don't know what's wrong. Can I blame it all on PMS?"

"You're a woman, so of course you can," I answered coyly.

"Any other time, I would have smacked you for that."

"You have a point. But it was you who brought it up. I just agreed."

Rebecca nodded as a slight smile pushed through the tears.

"Now come on. I need to get you back to bed."

I took Rebecca by the hand and helped her to her feet, supporting her arm as I led her out of the studio and back to the bedroom. Rebecca eased back onto the bed and I pulled the covers up and tucked her in.

"Now try to get some rest." I leaned over and kissed her. She latched onto my hand as I stared down at her. "I love you."

"I love you, too."

She released my hand as I reached over to turn the lamp off. Before stepping out of the room, I stopped in the doorway and looked back at Rebecca for a brief moment. I backed out of the room and returned to the studio. My path led me straight across the room to the window where I hoped against hope that this magical spot would relax me and reassure me that everything would be all right as I had told Rebecca moments earlier. I didn't know what we needed reassurance for or if there was even anything to worry about in the first place. Looking out into the blackness, the soothing sounds of the waves breaking on the shore lulled my mind. The only light came from high above where the full moon shimmered in the cloudless night, standing out from the backdrop of the multitudes of stars.

My gaze drifted from the darkness outside to the dim interior of the room. My wandering eyes came to rest on the unfinished painting, illuminated by the moonlight filtering through the window. I crossed the room to the portrait, sat down, and stared at the incomplete work. The still open tube of paint lay on the table in front of me. I screwed the lid back on, and then put the paints away before standing up and walking out of the studio back to the bedroom to try to salvage a few hours of sleep.

*   *   *

The early morning cries of seagulls rang through the air. A gentle breeze blew in through the open windows of the house. I scurried through the kitchen trying to fix a quick breakfast. A griddle with several strips of bacon sizzled on the stove next to a pan of steaming scrambled eggs. Two quick scoops later, the eggs were on two plates joined by the bacon. I set the plates on the kitchen table and poured two cups of coffee.

"Bec, breakfast is ready."

Pausing for a response, I stood there holding the cups. There was no answer. I set the cups on the table and walked back to the bedroom. Entering the room, I froze. The sight would forever haunt my memory. Rebecca lay sprawled out on the floor. My heart plunged through the depths of my body. I rushed across the room and fell to my knees beside her.

"No, please God! Bec!"

My finger grazed her cheek. Her skin felt warm and clammy. A faint, raspy cough escaped from her throat. I lifted her head and she began to stir.

"Martin?" she mumbled. "I don't feel so great."

"I need to get you to the hospital."

"No." Her voice came out in struggled breaths. "I don't want to go to the hospital."

I took her hand in my own and squeezed it. My other hand drifted up to her face and caressed her cheek.

"Please, Bec. Just let them have a look at you."

A sudden fit of coughing overtook Rebecca. She clutched her stomach. Her body convulsed with each escaping cough.

"Please, let me take you."

With the slightest nod of her head, Rebecca succumbed to my request. I grabbed a blanket from the bed and wrapped it around her. I gathered her in my arms and carried her out to the car, easing her down into the front seat and securing the seat belt around her. Time seemed to stand still as I sprinted to the other side of the car and hopped into the driver's seat. After a quick turn of the engine, I gunned the engine. The gas pedal hit the firewall and the car sped down the street.

Chapter Three

The silence of the hectic emergency room was as deafening as if it were a mallet pounding against the anvil of my head. I paced back and forth, up and down the checkerboard laminate floor. Where there should have been the echoes of my footsteps, I heard nothing but a muted silence. The persistently nagging feelings of worry and fear haunted my thoughts as I paced through the room.

A flash caught my eye and my gaze drifted down to the black and white tile floor. The flickering fluorescent lights reflected off of the buffed tiles. A sudden chill shot down through my body as I passed under the air vent, causing the small hairs on my neck to stand on end. It was no wonder people despised going to the hospital. The nauseating smell alone was enough to drive anyone insane. And insanity was exactly the brink on which I was teetering.

"Where is everyone?" I muttered aloud in disgust. The question repeated in my mind with every passing step. This was a hospital. There were supposed to be people here to help, to make you feel safe.

With each stride I grew more and more infuriated at the current situation and the lack of information I had. The image of my wife strewn on the floor in agony reverberated through my head. All I could think about was the worst possible scenario. Everything I should have said, but never did, began echoing through my mind. I wondered if I would still get the chance to say them or if the opportunity was forever lost to me now. Rebecca and I talked constantly, but I felt like kicking myself for each day that I could have said more to let her know how I felt.

I spun toward the front desk manned by a single receptionist busy with her own work. My pacing resumed. With every pass, I eyed the payphone in the corner of the room. Its silent voice called to me, trying to entice me to use it. I shook my head and continued pacing back and forth until I could no longer stand it. I made a beeline straight for the payphone, dropped in a few coins, and hurriedly punched in a number.

"Hey, it's me. I had to rush Bec to the hospital. I don't have a clue what's wrong. The doctor is still running tests. I don't know anything else, yet. I'll call you when I know more. Bye."

I hung up the phone and leaned back against the wall. A sudden rush of fatigue overtook my body. I looked around for the closest chair to collapse into. My eyes closed under the weight of the flood of thoughts that bombarded my mind, making me question everything in my life that I held dear. The dark prison held me for nearly two hours—which seemed like an eternity—until a door opened and a nurse walked into the waiting room, snapping me out of my daze. She stopped at the desk to talk to her colleague. I struggled to pull myself to my feet and walked up behind her. The desk phone rang, temporarily occupying the receptionist and giving me an opportunity to step in. I touched the unsuspecting nurse on the shoulder. She spun around in a whirl of white.

"Can I help you, sir?"

"I'm trying to find out about my wife. Rebecca Banks?"

"The doctor is still running tests on her."

"Will it be much longer?"

"It's hard to say, sir. But I can tell you that the doctor will be out as soon as possible to talk to you about his findings."

The nurse reached out and touched my arm as she offered a weary smile. A practiced effort, but still it worked. She then turned and walked down the hall, continuing her daily rounds. I stared after her as a door opened beside me. A middle-aged doctor wearing the typical white lab coat with glasses perched on the top of his head stepped out of a room and walked toward me.

"Mr. Banks? I'm Doctor Lankford," he announced, extending his hand to me.

I hesitated for a brief second before offering my hand to the doctor. "How's my wife?"

"That's what I wanted to talk to you about. We did blood work on your wife."

"Do you know what the problem is?"

"Well, in addition to the blood work, we did an MRI," the doctor continued. "As a result of the work done so far, we have discovered various abnormalities in her abdomen and ovaries."

"Abnormalities? What does that mean?"

"I'm not exactly sure at the moment. We would like to do exploratory surgery on her."

"How soon?"

"Dr. Wallace is in surgery right now, but as soon as he finishes with—"

Dr. Lankford's pager exuded a shrill beep from its spot on his belt. The doctor paused to look down at the message.

"Will you excuse me for a moment?"

I nodded at the doctor and then fell into the closest chair. Dr. Lankford picked up the phone from the front desk and punched in a few numbers. He spoke into the handset for a moment, adding a few animated gestures to emphasize his point, then hung up the phone and strode across the room toward me.

"I'm sorry about that. I have to go see a patient, but I wanted to let you know that the surgeon will be ready to proceed within the hour." The doctor paused for a moment. "And I'll send the resident who will be observing the surgery down and she can explain more about the procedure.

"Thank you."

Dr. Lankford acknowledged me with a slight nod then turned away and hurried down the hall toward the elevator. I watched him rush down the hall long enough to know he wasn't coming back anytime in the near future. Helplessness and fear rushed over me as I sat, eyes closed, with my head in my hands.

*   *   *

Shortly after talking to Dr. Lankford, I gave in to my fatigue and fell asleep. My head remained in my hands, too heavy to move. I awoke only long enough to talk to the resident. A few minutes after that, the surgeon stopped by my chair and I was able to hold Rebecca's hand for a few brief moments as she was wheeled to the operating room. Another restless, dreamless sleep caught me in its overwhelming grasp once they were gone. The feelings of helplessness and fear retook their dominating hold over my thoughts for the next two hours. Somewhere, calling deep from the darkness, a single voice rang out as if it were calling me back from the edge of nowhere.

"Martin, wake up." The soothing sound of a soft, feminine voice echoed through the empty blackness of my mind. "Martin!" The voice became more forceful and dominant as if just calling out wasn't enough for the hidden purpose it had. It seemed to be reaching out to me, breeching the void.

I felt a hand grab my arm and shake it just enough to pull me out of my restless sleep. My eyes opened, taking a moment to readjust to the fluorescent-lit waiting room. I looked beside me, half expecting to see another nurse or even the resident reporting back after the surgery, but instead Rebecca's younger sister was there.

"Kelly?" I stared at her. My lips formed the words but no sound came out. It took a moment before I was able to speak. "What are you doing here?"

"I was really worried because your message didn't give much information as to what was wrong."

"So you just up and drove here? It's almost a four hour drive from Greenville."

"A little over three when properly motivated."

"But still…" I trailed off.

"My sister is suddenly rushed to the hospital and no one knows what's wrong. What am I supposed to do—stay at home and act like everything is okay?"

There was nothing more for me to say. I knew the only possible response was to smile and nod. Having known Kelly nearly as long as I had known Rebecca, I had plenty of insight into her personality and how to deal with her strong-willed intricacies. She was not the type of person to hold back, or hide, what she was thinking. The expression "wears her heart on her sleeve" seemed to have been coined specifically for her. Kelly was one of the most giving and most caring people that I had ever met, evidenced by her dropping everything to make the trip here, which was not an easy task considering she had three kids of her own at home.

"So what's been going on?" Kelly asked. The subtle intensity of her brown eyes pushed through my natural defenses.

"Nothing out of the ordinary. At least nothing that I can think of." I scanned my mind to see if there was anything that I might have missed. "I went into the bedroom and found her on the floor. It all happened so suddenly," I trailed off as the memory of finding Rebecca on the floor consumed my thoughts.

"I meant in general. As in what's been going on the past couple of months since the last time I was here. I've hardly talked to Bec in the last two weeks at all."

"Oh." I answered with my best attempt at a save. "I knew that."

"I'm sure you did."

"Bec's been really busy at the store, at least up until two weeks ago. It's been the usual for the most part, other than she took some time off because her back had been hurting."

"What did she do to it?"

"Wasn't really sure. She had a store inventory last month. It started hurting not long after that."

"Why didn't she go to the doctor?"

"I tried to get her to, but she was really swamped at the shop. And she thought she just pulled something during the inventory. That's why she took so much time off the past couple of weeks. Besides, you know your sister and doctors."

"She should have still gone at the first sign of pain."

"A mother's instinct?"

"Maybe so," Kelly shrugged. No stranger to hospitals and doctors' offices herself, Kelly had her share of cuts, scrapes, illnesses, and various other ailments with her three kids. "So what about you?"

"What about me?"

"What have you been up to lately?"

"The same old stuff. You should know by now that I'm pretty set in my routine."

"I know, I know, but I keep thinking that you just might somehow surprise me one of these days."

"Don't hold your breath." The faintest of smiles squeezed past my lips for the first time the whole day. It felt good to actually smile, but the ever-present feeling of guilt for smiling during a situation like this clouded my face.

Kelly sprang to her feet and looked up and down the hall. "I need some coffee. Is there anywhere around here that I can get a decent cup?"

Blinking a few times, I shook my head to clear the fuzziness. "Yeah," I answered, "down the hall and around the corner, in the cafeteria."

"Great, do you want anything?"

"Oh, sure. Coffee would be nice."

"Well, I'll be back in a minute."

Kelly took off down the hall. I straightened up in the chair as I watched her leave, only to slouch back down when she vanished around the corner. The shocked feeling from when I opened my eyes and saw Kelly sitting there still remained, though not as strong, and it was being replaced with a sense of peace and calmness from her presence. I let my head lean back against the wall and closed my eyes for the few minutes that Kelly would be gone. She returned with two cups of coffee in hand and sat back down beside me.

"Careful," she said, handing me one of the cups. "It's hot."

"Thanks." I took the cup with both hands, raised it to my lips, and blew on the steaming liquid.

"When was the last time you ate anything?"

I looked down at my wrist, but saw only the telltale tan line where my watch should have been. "I don't know. Dinner last night, I guess."

Kelly nodded at me before responding. "I noticed some decent looking food in the cafeteria when I was getting the coffee. I was quite surprised, this being a hospital and all."

I cocked my head and smiled at Kelly as I forced out a hushed laugh.

"Well, I'm kind of hungry," she continued. "If I went to get something, would you join me?"

"Yeah, sure, I'll go. But do you think it's a good idea to leave?"

"I'll let the desk know where we'll be, so they can find us if they need to."

Kelly offered a sympathetic smile and squeezed my arm. She hopped up from the chair and walked over to the desk. The mumbled conversation between her and the receptionist lasted just a few short words. She returned to where I sat, grabbed my hand, and pulled me to my feet.

Within five minutes, we both sat at a table in the corner of the cafeteria. Two fresh cups of steaming coffee and two trays of food sat on the table in front of us. I took a bite of my sandwich and set it back on the plate as I chewed with a distant thoughtfulness. Kelly sat across from me, her food still untouched on the plate.

"How are you really doing?"

I stopped chewing and looked at her for a moment. The food in my mouth provided a welcome distraction for a few seconds. I swallowed the mouthful of sandwich and dabbed at my lips with the napkin.

"I'm not really sure how to answer that."

"What do you mean?" Kelly leaned forward and rested her elbows on the table.

"I don't really know. I mean, everything in me wants to believe that this is nothing. That the doctor is going to come out and say that nothing's wrong and I can take her home." My eyes wandered around the room as I paused for a minute to gather my thoughts. "But there's the smallest thought that keeps nagging me, screaming out that something's really wrong."

"I know how you feel. I've felt that way since I got your call this morning."

"I just don't know how to feel—or what to do, for that matter."

I dropped my head into my hands and slumped forward in the chair, defeated. Kelly slid her chair around the table to sit next to me. She slipped her arm around me and rested her head on my shoulder.

* * *

At a quarter to seven, the surgeon, Dr. Carter Wallace, came out into the waiting room to talk to us. After introducing himself to Kelly and me, the three of us stood there in a moment of awkward silence before I leaned forward and spoke.

"So how is my wife, Doctor?"

The doctor said nothing to answer my question. He just gestured toward an open door down the hall. "There's a room waiting where we can go and talk that affords a little privacy." He paused. "So if you'll follow me."

He led us the few steps down the hall and into the closet-sized room. Kelly and I sat down on the small couch as the doctor sat in the chair across from us. The temperature seemed to rise twenty degrees in as many seconds, compounding my already nervous state of mind.

"Your wife is resting in the recovery room now. She's still under the effects of the anesthetic, so it will be a while before she wakes up."

"When will we be able to see her?"

"As I said, she's still asleep, but there's no reason you couldn't go in and sit with her."

Both Kelly and I leaned back on the couch, slightly relaxed. Dr. Wallace leaned forward closer to us.

"Before you go in to see her, there's something you should know," he stated.

I glanced over at Kelly, who was looking right back at me, then turned again toward the doctor.

"What is it?"

"As you're aware, Dr. Lankford did preliminary blood work and an MRI and found some abnormalities in her abdomen and ovaries. That's why we went ahead with the exploratory surgery."

"So what does all that mean?" I leaned forward, unsure of whether I actually wanted an answer to my question.

"We found cancer in your wife's ovaries, and it has already spread to the liver."

I stared at him in complete shock. I couldn't believe the

words he'd just spoken. All feeling drained from my limbs. My elbow slipped off of my knee. I managed to grab the arm of the couch to regain my balance and prevent a face plant to the floor. The air rushed out of my lungs.

"H-how can that be? She seemed fine, except for a little soreness in her back."

Dr. Wallace scratched his chin before answering. "One of the tumors was very near the L4 Lumbar. Any pressure in that area could have explained the lower back pain." His eyebrows scrunched together as he remained quiet for a moment before continuing. "Did she have any complaints such as fatigue, shortness of breath, lack of appetite, or nausea?"

I leaned back and rubbed my chin. Various instances popped into my mind as I tried to remember any specific times. They all flooded back in an instant—the walk on the beach when she got tired, and all the meals I fixed that she hardly touched. "Yeah, she did," I mumbled. "Um, there were times she…when Rebecca, couldn't eat. And when she did, she couldn't hold it down. And lately, she got tired really easily."

"Yes, that would be consistent with the diagnosis," Dr. Wallace commented as he looked down at the chart in his hands.

"Excuse me? You come out and tell me that my wife has cancer…and this stuff is all consistent?"

"I'm sorry, Mr. Banks. I didn't mean to upset you."

"Well, tell me, Doctor," I glared at the man. Uncontrollable fury burned its way up the side of my neck. "How exactly would you feel if you were in my place?"

I inched forward in my seat closer to Dr. Wallace as the anger swelled inside me. Kelly grabbed my arm and eased me back. She caressed my arm, consoling me, calming me down as if I were one of her anxious children.

"Why is this just being found out now?" Kelly asked the doctor.

Dr. Wallace shook his head. "I can't really answer that. There wasn't anything in her previous medical history that even remotely offered that something was wrong."

Kelly dropped her head and frowned, echoing my sentiment that this was an unavoidable medical mystery. "Shouldn't something have been discovered during her checkup?"

"Ideally, that's what we hope for. But realistically, it's just not the case. There's no prudent method for checking for ovarian cancer, such as a mammogram screen for breast cancer. We only catch about twenty-five percent of cases in the early stages."

"What about a pap smear?" Kelly retorted. "Isn't that designed to detect cancerous cells?"

"It is. But it was designed to detect cervical cancer, not ovarian. Most of the time, the changes undergone due to ovarian cancer are rarely picked up during a checkup."

"What can you do for her?" I asked as I struggled to pull myself up in the couch. "Chemotherapy?"

"That's definitely one of the options. I was unable to remove the majority of the tumors safely. Hopefully, we can find a way to shrink them down enough so they can be removed surgically."

"You said one of the options?" Kelly repeated.

"The three main options are surgery, chemotherapy, and radiation therapy, or a combination of the last two," Dr. Wallace explained. "Surgery isn't feasible at the moment, at least not until the tumors have decreased in size and are more accessible."

"Can you explain them to us?" she requested.

"Of course. Surgery is going in to physically cut out the objects. Radiation therapy is like an x-ray, just in a much higher dose. It's designed to kill the cancerous cells and shrink the tumors prior to surgery. It can be administered either externally or internally directly to the cancer sites. And finally, chemotherapy is the use of medications or chemicals having the ability to fight the cancer."

"What do you think is the best choice for us?" I asked.

Dr. Wallace looked over at me for a second before answering. "If it were up to me, I would go with radiation therapy. That's the best option, because it is applied directly to the cancer site."

"Then let's start that immediately."

"We will have to wait until Rebecca wakes up. I need to talk with her before making any final decisions."

"But she's my wife. If something can be done to help, I want that done."

"I understand that. Believe me. But your wife is not in a coma, or on life support, so the choice must be hers as to how we proceed."

I could do nothing but shake my head in disgust. The fact that I was her husband should account for something. I should at least be able to make decisions that might help her.

"I have to inform you," Dr. Wallace said. "Your wife is in Stage IV, the most advanced stage of ovarian cancer. The cancer is in both ovaries and has spread to the liver. We also found cancer cells in the pleural fluid, the cavity that surrounds the lungs."

"Then what's her prognosis, Doctor?" Kelly jumped in.

"It will all depend on how she reacts to the radiation therapy. Right now, she has six months, at the most." He glanced down at the floor as if searching for something more to say. "But there are new treatment programs being developed every day."

Fighting to contain my composure, my entire body collapsed in shock. Kelly's grip on my arm grew tighter. Her nails dug into the tender flesh of my arm. The sudden and abrupt revelation floored both of us. The tears welled up in my eyes. After a brief pause, the floodgates opened and the tears streamed down my cheeks. Kelly fell back into the couch, crying as well. Dr. Wallace slowly stood up.

"I'll let you be alone now. If you need me, the front desk can call me," Dr. Wallace said before walking out of the room. He paused in the doorway. "And once again, I'm very sorry."

"Doctor," I called out as he started to step into the hall. "Can we see her now?"

The doctor nodded then disappeared around a corner. Kelly and I sat frozen in our chairs, both sobbing and unable to move.

Chapter Four

The recovery room loomed in front of me like an imposing dark and gloomy prison that was dimly lit by only a few fluorescent tracks above the beds. Kelly and I crept silently past the other beds. A narrow oxygen tube looped around Rebecca's ears, feeding the purified air through the nosepiece. The piercing sight of the IV in her hand brought an onset of horrifying thoughts that no one should ever have to experience about a person they love. That sight alone caused my eyes to well up with tears again. Waging the losing battle with my building emotions, I crossed the room and stood at the foot of Rebecca's bed. Kelly eased down in the chair beside the headboard. I watched in silence as Rebecca's chest rose and fell methodically with each passing breath. The nearby monitor emitted a constant beeping as it monitored her heartbeat.

I stepped forward next to Kelly and fell to my knees beside the bed, my fingers intertwining with Rebecca's. I buried my face down in the bed with my head resting against the point of her hip. Without saying a word, Kelly leaned forward and caressed my shoulder. Except for the muffled sounds of my crying, we both sat in complete silence until a nurse entered the room to check on Rebecca a few minutes later. I stood beside Kelly's chair and watched while the nurse did her job. After completing her tasks, she turned to leave the room. Kelly jumped out of her chair and crossed the room to catch the nurse before she left, leaving me alone to watch their conversation from beside the bed.

"How long do you think it will be before she wakes up?"

"It's hard to say. My best estimate is a couple hours, or it could really be anytime. It depends on her."

The nurse offered a forced smile before she turned and checked on the other patients in the room. Kelly remained standing there in silence until long after the nurse disappeared behind another curtain. Sometime during her talk with the nurse, I pulled myself into the chair and stared at Rebecca. A sense of calmness surrounded her, no signs of nervousness or worry. It seemed as if nothing was wrong with her, as if she would wake up at any moment and everything would be back as it should be.

"It's probably going to be another two hours before she wakes up. Why don't you go home, get cleaned up, and grab something to eat."

"I don't want to leave her," I responded emotionlessly as Kelly kneeled down in front of me.

"I understand that, I really do. But there's nothing you can do for her until she wakes up and I'll stay here the whole time. So she won't be alone."

"You know what happened to my father's first wife, so you should know why I won't leave." Kelly stared up at me as I retold the story. "She was in for routine surgery. One of the nurses suggested that he go home to change and grab dinner before she got out of the operating room. So that's what he did. While he was gone, she had an aneurism on the table. The hospital called him at home and he rushed back, but it was too late. She died before he got back, all alone with no one there to be with her. My dad never forgave himself for leaving."

"I'm sorry. I should have remembered that." Kelly took my hand in hers. "And I can see why you don't want to leave, believe me. But this is different. She's not in surgery where something can go wrong. She's already out and just waiting to wake up. If it makes any difference, she won't be alone at all. I am going to sit here with her the entire time until you get back. I won't even get up from this chair."

"I don't know. I just can't get past the thought that if I leave, something could happen."

"Look, I promise that nothing will happen. I'll be here the whole time. And I mean this in the nicest possible way, but you look horrible. You don't want Bec to wake up and find you looking like that, do you?" She pointed at me as I looked down. My clothes were completely disheveled. I could only imagine how my face looked.

Instead of answering I just shook my head. As much as I hated to admit it, she did have a valid point.

"So then go," she begged with a little more push in her tone. "I'll be here the whole time and I promise that I'll call you if she wakes up."

Though I was still very hesitant to leave, Kelly was even more adamant when it came to things of importance. I finally relented, leaving Kelly sitting beside the bed, and shuffled out of the room and down the eerie hospital corridors.

* * *

It was nearly eight by the time I pulled in front of the house. The drive passed by with excruciating slowness, nothing but me alone with my thoughts. My mind raced back and forth. Everything that was not Rebecca retreated into the dark depths of my mind. The familiar sights outside the window blurred together. The views that I loved so much became indistinguishable. That I made it home in one piece was a small miracle.

I parked the car and slid out of the seat. I froze in front of the house, gazing up at the blackness of night. Not a single cloud blotted the sky. The nearly full moon glowed overhead, casting its soft light down to illuminate the path to our house. On any other night, Rebecca and I would sit on the porch swing together curled up beneath a blanket for hours just staring out over the water, watching the rippling of the moonlight across the surface, or listening to the unseen waves crashing along the beach. Sometimes we would talk, while other times we would be content to sit quietly in each other's company. The views had always been so peaceful, so serene. No matter what had happened that particular day, it would be forgotten for those few precious hours spent together on the swing. I prayed with all my being to be able to wake up from this maddening dream and have Rebecca walk out the front door to join me.

I walked up the stairs and paused on the porch. The wooden swing called to me from the corner of my eye. Hesitantly, I stepped closer and closer, caught under the spell of night, and sat down. The old chain links groaned and creaked as the swing glided back and forth. Pale white streaks of light glistened off of the breaking whitecaps and cast a glare across my eyes as the tears began to well up no matter how hard I tried to fight them.

"Why are You letting this happen?" My eyes searched the black horizon as if waiting for an audible answer, but a mocking silence was my only response.

When nothing happened, I became even more upset. The chains on the swing buckled as I sprang to my feet, grabbed the railing, and began yelling toward the sky. "Why would You take her from me? She's never done anything. Take anything else You want. Anything." The words struggled out of my mouth. "Take me instead, just don't take her."

Fatigue washed over my body, pounding me with the relentless fury of the storm-tossed sea. I collapsed back on the swing and stared through unseeing eyes. The will to fight any longer completely left me. The words came out in a whisper. "Please, don't take her away from me, not like this. She's my life. What am I supposed to do without her?"

The crash of the breaking waves on the shoreline punctuated the conclusion of my pleading prayer. My gaze refocused on the rippling water for a moment before I stood up and moved toward the front door. The clicking of the tumblers echoed through the night as the key slid into the lock. The door swung open, illuminating the foyer with the dim rays filtering through the doorway. My imposing shadow filled the entire hallway like a faithful sentry blocking my path from entering.

A strange feeling passed over me as I stood on the porch looking down the darkened hall. Nervousness and anxiety began to build up in the awkward pause. For the first time ever, I didn't want to enter my own house. The horrifying image of finding Rebecca tore through my mind in a brutal rampage. Everything inside of me begged to just close the door and head back to the hospital to be by her side when she woke up. After a great deal of effort and persuasion, I pushed through the fears and my feet shuffled forward, inch by inch, through the doorway and into the house.

I inched through the darkness to the kitchen and reached out for the light switch. The fluorescent lights flickered on, bathing the room with light. The kitchen remained exactly as I left it earlier that morning. Two plates of eggs still sat on the table; the once-sizzling bacon had long since cooled; the two cups of coffee were now cold. I grabbed the plates and scraped the food into the trash can and then set them in the sink. I poured the coffee down the drain and set the cups on top of the plates. After looking around the kitchen for a minute, I stepped back and inched toward the bedroom. I paused just before I got to the open door not knowing what to expect when I stepped into the room. My eyes closed and I took slow, deep breaths to calm myself before entering. The blinds were still drawn, engulfing the room in complete blackness. I reached for the light switch and flipped it on. The bed remained unmade, sheets dangling, half-lying in a pile on the floor. The memory of entering the room and finding Rebecca crumpled on the floor rushed back into my mind. I squeezed my eyes shut in an attempt to force out the images as I stumbled into the bathroom.

The steaming water cascaded over my body in a failed attempt to relax and forget about everything for the moment. After drying off, I got dressed as fast as possible, glancing at the clock as I grabbed a shirt—just past eight-thirty. Stepping out of the bedroom, I stopped in the hallway and stared up and down the hall feeling completely lost. The half-open door to the studio called to me. Taking small, unsure steps, I crept toward the door. The room beckoned me to enter. Somehow I resisted the urge, content to look inside as the moonlight filtered in through the window. The unfinished portrait sat on the easel, gazing back at me. Its words resounded in my head. "Finish me, Martin." I was unable to withstand the calling any longer and stepped through the threshold. My gaze locked longingly onto Rebecca's eyes. With no attempt to control my emotions, I broke down and sobbed in front of the portrait.

"What am I supposed to do without you? You're my life, my soul. I have nothing without you. I am nothing without you."

Instinctively, my hand reached out for the canvas, tracing the contours of the rough fabric and stopping just short of the painted areas. A sudden rush of cool air blew in through the open window. I jerked my hand away from the easel and my eyes darted around the room. Rebecca's eyes seemed to follow my gaze as I peered through the shadow-filled room. I backed away from the painting. Through the darkness, Rebecca's eyes seemed locked on me as I retreated out of the room and quietly closed the door behind me.

Chapter Five

It was almost ten by the time I arrived back at the hospital. It had been longer than the two hours and I hoped that Rebecca had not woken up yet since I desperately wanted to be there when she did, to be the first person she saw. The nervous feeling began working its way back into my body as my steps echoed along the corridor to the recovery room. Entering the room, the curtain around Rebecca's bed hid the top half of her body. A small light behind the bed cast a dim luminescence over the space and covered the curtain with shadows. I could hear Kelly's voice whispering from the other side of the room. Not wanting to interrupt, I waited out of sight behind the curtain to give Kelly time to finish talking. Though I tried not to listen I couldn't help but hear the conversation.

"I don't really know what I'm going to do with that boy. The other day he found a snakeskin somewhere in the neighborhood and decided he would bring it home to add to his collection. I was downstairs cooking and went to tell the kids to clean up for dinner. When I walked into his room, he's playing a video game. I opened the desk drawer to put the game away so we could get cleaned up, and he had the snake-skin curled up in the drawer. I nearly had a heart attack. I thought he learned his lesson about bringing things like that home last month when he put a frog in his pocket, which, of course, he forgot about. I happened to find it when I was doing the laundry. But he is only eight years old. What can you expect?"

I caught the laugh just before it escaped my mouth. Several weeks earlier, Rebecca had told me about the story of Kelly finding the frog. The silence lingered on the other side of the curtain and I decided it was safe to go in and interrupt. I eased the curtain open a little farther and stepped in. Kelly looked up at me, her eyes glistening with tears in the dim light.

"Are you okay?"

"I'm fine," she replied, wiping her eyes as she stood up. "Did you get something to eat?"

"I wasn't hungry, but I got cleaned up."

"Good."

"Have you eaten yet?"

"No, I didn't want to leave her alone." Her hand drifted to her stomach. "I am getting a little hungry, though."

"Why don't you go get something to eat? I'll sit with her until you get back."

Kelly nodded and rose to her feet. I stepped out of her way to allow her to move though the small space. She paused for a second as she passed by and reached out to squeeze my arm. Once she left, I collapsed in the chair next to Rebecca's bed and took her hand in mine.

After ten minutes of sitting, Rebecca began to stir. Her skin looked pale and clammy as her head slowly moved from side to side. She eased open her eyes and looked around the room.

Rebecca managed an audible whisper. "Martin."

"Hey, baby, how are you feeling?"

"Terrible."

"I know, honey." Words suddenly left me. I struggled for something, anything, to say. "I talked to the doctor. He said that…he said that you were going to be all right."

A faint twinkle came to her eye as she called me out. "You never were much of a liar." She motioned toward a cup of water on the table. "Can you give me that?"

I grabbed the cup from the table and handed it to her. She struggled to pull herself up in the bed then she took the cup from me and sipped the water.

"Is that better?"

Rebecca nodded and handed me the cup, but didn't speak. The look in her eyes told me all I needed to know. She knew exactly what was happening, exactly what was going on. My mouth opened, as if to speak, but no words came out. My mind went as blank as a slate. I figured Rebecca understood what was happening in my head because she looked over at me and took my hand, interlacing her fingers in mine.

"I had the weirdest dream while I was asleep. I dreamt that Kelly came to visit and was telling me about some of the crazy things Sean had been doing."

"Oh really?" I played along, not wanting to tell her that it wasn't a dream yet. "What else happened?"

"I'm not really sure. It was something about him bringing home animals, or something, leaving them in his dresser."

I smiled at Rebecca's retelling of her dream because I knew it was true, and she was remembering the story that Kelly had told her earlier. I wanted to tell her about Kelly, but I held off, deciding to surprise Rebecca when Kelly came back from eating. Rebecca and I just sat there without speaking. We were just content to be in each other's presence. The company itself was enough.

Even though the curtain was still partially closed, I had a clear view of the door, so I saw when Kelly returned from the cafeteria. She paused outside the curtain to give me a few more minutes alone with my wife.

"Oh, I forgot to tell you," I said, preparing her for the surprise. "You had a visitor while you were asleep."

I always found it funny that when you informed someone they had a visitor they always looked around the room even when they knew it was empty. Rebecca could see that we were the only people in the curtained off area, but she still looked around as if expecting to see someone else all of a sudden.

"Who was it? It wasn't Mary Walters, was it? I wouldn't be surprised if she had already heard and showed up just to check on me."

"No, it wasn't her."

"Well, who was it? Just tell me."

Before answering, I looked toward the break in the curtain. Kelly stepped forward through the opening and stopped at the foot of the bed. Rebecca turned her head and her jaw dropped when she saw Kelly standing in front of her.

"Hey, hon. Glad to see you're finally awake."

Rebecca stared up at her sister. "What are you doing here?"

"Martin called me this morning and I drove down."

"You didn't have to do that, but I'm glad you're here."

Kelly walked around the bed and stopped next to Rebecca. She looked down at her sister and smiled as she took her hand.

"So when do I get out of here? I just want to go home."

My eyes locked on Kelly for a moment before returning to Rebecca. I knew I had to tell her what Dr. Wallace told us. I leaned forward, still holding Rebecca's hand, and began telling her what I was told a few hours prior. Kelly sat down on the opposite side of the bed and held Rebecca's other hand. We spent the next twenty minutes recounting the conversation with the doctor and discussing what the possible options were. I realized that the conversation was not what I had expected when Rebecca didn't seem to be shocked at the revelation of her condition. It was almost as if she knew. The biggest surprise came from her response when I finished talking.

"When do we go home?" she asked again.

For a second I just stared at her, thinking that maybe she didn't understand what I had just said. But I soon realized she understood completely.

"I just want to go home, Martin. I don't want to be in a hospital. I want to be at home…with you."

I leaned closer to her and lost myself in her eyes. It took all of my strength to hold together and remain strong. "No matter where you are, that's where I'll be."

"I know."

"I'll go talk to the doctor and see what we can do."

I kissed Rebecca and held her in a tender embrace for the longest time before stepping through the curtain on my way out of the room. My footsteps echoed along the desolate halls as I made my way toward the nurse's station to ask for Dr. Wallace. The nurse informed me that he was in the middle of rounds, but she would page him. I sat down in the waiting room, figuring it would give Kelly and Rebecca time to talk on their own. A few minutes later, Dr. Wallace walked down the hall toward me. I rose to greet him as he approached.

"Dr. Wallace."

"How are you doing? Is there anything I can do for you?"

"I just wanted to know when it would be possible to take Rebecca home. I know she probably needs to stay overnight for observation at least, but when would it be possible?"

"Honestly, it would depend on how she is feeling. She will have to stay overnight for observation, like you anticipated. I might consider releasing her tomorrow, if she seems to be doing well enough. But it's something that the three of us will have to discuss further at that time. There are still decisions that must be made regarding how to proceed with treatment."

I gave Dr. Wallace a half-attempted smile and extended my hand toward him. "Thank you, Doctor."

"It's no problem, Mr. Banks." He held my gaze for a moment before continuing. "I would like to suggest one thing, that you call hospice. They can help you with her care once you get her home."

"I'll look into that, thanks."

"Well, I need to check on a few more patients. As for taking her home, I will stop by tomorrow afternoon and see if we can start the process of discharging her. A nurse will be down in a few minutes to check on her and move her to a room. I'll be in to check on her after that."

I nodded in acknowledgement. Dr. Wallace turned and walked back down the hall. I sat down in one of the many empty chairs in the waiting room and contemplated the recent events in my life. After a few minutes of fervent prayer, I got up and walked back into the recovery room to rejoin Kelly and Rebecca. The two women were engaged in conversation as I entered the room. I took a seat in the corner and listened.

The nurse soon came in to check on Rebecca again in

preparation of moving her to a private room. With relative ease for such a petite nurse, she wheeled Rebecca's bed out of the room and down the hallway toward the elevator. The three of us settled down in a second floor room. The nurse brought in a small cot for Kelly while we waited for the doctor to return. Due to the lack of space in the room, I settled for one of the chairs and began trying to get situated for what I assumed would be a long, uncomfortable night. Dr. Wallace entered the room a few minutes later and did a quick check of Rebecca. He bid us goodnight after finishing and disappeared back into the hallway.

Chapter Six

The rumble of the bustling hospital pressed through the deep reaches of my fitful sleep. Even through the closed door, the passing of nurses, doctors and patients filtered into the room. The squeaking of wheelchairs and gurneys rolling down the hallway drew me out of my restless sleep. As my eyes opened and began adjusting to the light, Kelly crossed the room and knelt down beside me.

"I was about to wake you up. I brought you some coffee. The pot just finished brewing as I got there."

I took the cup from her and blew on the liquid before taking my first sip. Rejuvenated and instantly awakened by the onset of the caffeine rush, I perked up in my seat and looked around the room. Rebecca was still asleep in her bed.

"She woke up about an hour ago. But I managed to convince her to go back to sleep."

I nodded and took another sip of the steaming coffee. It was a laborious and painful struggle to pull myself to my feet, but as I stood beside the bed, gazing down at Rebecca as she slept, the pain faded away. She looked so peaceful, so content, as if there was nothing in the world that could bother her. Perhaps as a result of the sedatives and pain killers, for the first time in over a month Rebecca had gotten a good night's sleep. As I stood over her, I lost all comprehension of time.

One of the countless nurses slipped into the room to do a quick check on Rebecca. I was so focused on my wife that I didn't even notice the nurse until she was done. As she headed toward the door to leave, I stopped her to ask about the status of Rebecca's discharge. The nurse told me that Dr. Wallace would be down soon to make his decision and then she left the room to continue on her rounds. I sat back down next to Rebecca and once again took her hand in mine as I leaned over to kiss her cheek. Kelly sat down by the door to give Rebecca and me an opportunity to talk.

"Are you sure this is what you want to do?"

"I'm positive." The fire of determination burned in her eyes. "I want to be with you at home, Martin."

That was all I needed to hear from her. No matter what she wanted, I would do everything in my power to see that she got it. I leaned closer to her and stared into her eyes. It took all my strength to hold together and remain strong, a task that was becoming increasingly harder to pull off. "I'll see what I can do."

I wrapped my arms around Rebecca and held her in a long embrace. Finally, I stood up and turned toward the door. Dr. Wallace stood beside Kelly, who rose from her chair and moved toward the seat I just vacated. I crossed the room and extended my hand to him.

"Doctor, I didn't know you were here."

"I slipped in a minute ago." He turned his attention to Rebecca. "Let's see how she's doing today." Dr. Wallace crossed the room and began checking Rebecca, starting with the incision just below her waistline. After inspecting the stitches and making sure there was no infection, he compared the chart and the IV. When he finished the checkup, he took me to the side while Kelly sat with Rebecca. "I heard you talking about not wanting to stay in the hospital. Can I talk to you outside for a second?"

I nodded as we made our way through the door and into the hall. "Is taking her home going to be a problem?"

"In your case, I don't see where that would be. I would like to suggest one thing again, that you look into involving hospice in the near future. They can help make everything much easier and more convenient for you."

"How exactly would that work?"

"Hospice is an organization that focuses on palliative treatment, rather than curative. That just means that they come in to take care of the patient and make them comfortable, as opposed to trying to cure them. In your case, someone from hospice would come two or three times a week to check on your wife and give medicine and any other helpful treatments. The visit would only be for an hour or two on the days they come. It's just mainly so that you don't have to do all of this yourself. So that you have help and can focus on other, more important matters, such as your wife, instead of her treatment."

I nodded as he explained hospice, soaking in all the information he offered. It sounded helpful to me, but my mind refused to stay focused on his words. I glanced back at the door to Rebecca's room then extended my hand toward him. "Thank you, Doctor, we really appreciate it."

"It's the least I can do. I'll get started on the paperwork to have her discharged."

As I stepped through the door into the room, a smile came to my face for the first time in what seemed like a year, though it had really just been the past day. I stared across the room at Rebecca, engrossed in a conversation with Kelly. Dr. Wallace still stood just outside the door.

"I'll send down a nurse in a few minutes who will explain some of the procedures that you will need to know. If you'll excuse me."

"Thank you," I replied, sitting down in the chair beside the door. The weight of the world resting on my shoulders was far too much for any one person to bear. The feelings of loneliness and doubt rushed over me and my eyes grew heavy. With little resistance, they started to fall shut as my head leaned back against the wall. I drifted off into an uneasy blackness as I waited for the nurse.

*   *   *

The double sliding doors slid apart and a young orderly pushed Rebecca's wheelchair out into the brisk afternoon air, flanked on one side by me, holding my wife's hand, and on the other side by Kelly. The orderly stopped short of the curb and locked the brakes on the wheelchair. I jogged out into the parking lot to retrieve the car and pulled to a stop a few feet in front of Rebecca. Nothing the whole day had made me feel like I did at that very moment—I was returning home with the woman I loved, escaping from the clutches of the hospital. I jumped out of the car and hurried around the vehicle to open the passenger door. With help from both Kelly and the orderly, Rebecca rose to her feet and eased down into the seat. I thanked the orderly. He offered a smile then retrieved the wheelchair and disappeared back inside the building. Before sliding back into the driver's seat, I turned to Kelly.

"Is your car close?"

"Yeah, it's just over there." She pointed to the lot I just returned from.

"Oh, okay. We're going straight home."

"Well, I'll get the car and follow you back."

I nodded and slid back behind the wheel. Kelly rushed across the parking lot to her car. I waited until she fell in behind us before pulling away from the curb. We pulled out of the lot and merged into the light traffic. I glanced over and spied Rebecca with the slightest grin on her face.

"What's that for?"

"What?"

"You're smiling."

Rebecca stared through the side window as the hospital grew smaller behind us. "I'm just happy to be going home." She turned her head and smiled at me.

I reciprocated her smile then returned my focus to the road in front of us. Rebecca watched me for a second and then resumed gazing out of the window at the landscape.

* * *

The monotonous forty-five minute drive home seemed to last for hours. The scenery passed by rather slowly and every few minutes I found myself checking the rear view mirror to make sure Kelly was still behind us. The news of Rebecca's prognosis was still sinking in. My mind raced at what the possibilities were. I wanted nothing more than to return home, run straight into our room, and crawl in bed if it meant that I could wake up from this horrible nightmare.

The twenty-four hour ordeal at the hospital had taken a serious toll on both of us and was not appearing to be letting up anytime soon. I glanced down at my watch as I got out of the car—a little after noon. As I circled around the car to the passenger door to help Rebecca to her feet, Kelly pulled into the driveway and parked behind us. Rebecca looped her arm around mine and we inched our way up the steps. Kelly jumped out of her car and hurried to catch up with us, taking my keys to unlock the door. The events of a little more than a day prior flooded into my head again just as they did the night before. I helped Rebecca to the couch so she could lie down and then stepped into the kitchen to fix drinks for the three of us. Kelly sat down next to Rebecca as I left. I searched through the refrigerator for something to drink. I filled three glasses with sweet tea and took two of them in to Rebecca and Kelly.

"Here you go." I handed one glass to Rebecca and the other to Kelly before returning to the kitchen to grab my own glass. A moment later, I rejoined Rebecca and Kelly in the living room.

Rebecca stared at the drink. She took a quick sip of the cool liquid and smiled over at me as I sat down across from her. "Thank you."

The three of us sat in silence for a while. No words were needed. We were content to just ponder our own thoughts while sipping our tea. After a while, Kelly made a comment that started the ball rolling. As soon as one topic was exhausted, another immediately took its place. As the minutes turned into hours, Rebecca began to drop out of the conversation and curled up on the couch beside me. Four hours later, Kelly excused herself and disappeared into the kitchen to fix dinner. I popped in every so often to help but kept being sent back to the couch. Kelly ended up raiding the leftovers in the fridge and brought the plates to us a few minutes later. The three of us ate in an uneasy silence.

When the meal was over I began to retrieve the dishes but was promptly reprimanded by Kelly. She took the plates and told me that she would take care of cleaning up. Not used to being forbidden from cooking in my own house, I plopped back down on the couch. Rebecca shifted around to rest her head on my lap. An old afghan that my mother had knitted shortly after Rebecca's and my wedding rested on the back of the couch. I reached up and pulled it from its spot and tucked it around my wife. My gaze wandered around the room before resting on the view of the moonlit ocean out of the window. The sea, although always changing, was constant, always there. It was my rock, my strength. There would never be a day when I looked out of my window to find that the ocean was no longer there. My gaze broke from the water every few minutes to look down at Rebecca, now sleeping. Her hair glowed in the soft light. Every so often, I caught myself as my fingers ran through her hair.

Those few minutes quickly turned into two hours. Kelly had long since finished cleaning up the kitchen and had taken her bags into the guest room without disturbing us on the couch. She remained back in the room, out of sight, giving us time to be alone. I glanced over at the clock and was shocked to see how late it was. Carefully, so as not to disturb Rebecca, I slipped off of the couch, scooped her up in my arms, and carried her back to our bedroom. She never stirred during the short trip. I tucked her in bed and kissed her on the cheek then sat down in the chair next to the bed. The room was dark, save for the soft, dim light filtering in from the hallway. There was just enough light for me to sit and watch my wife sleep.

Chapter Seven

The muffled sound of a bird shrieking outside the window jarred me out of a light sleep. My eyes adjusted to the faint light filtering through the curtains. A roaring fire seared through my neck as I sat up in the chair a little too quickly, but all the physical pain faded away in an instant when my eyes fell on Rebecca, sound asleep, curled up under the blankets.

I stood up and attempted to massage out the kinks as I walked to the kitchen. The curtains in the living room were pulled aside, bathing the room in light. Thursday's mid-morning sun peeked out from behind a cover of billowing white clouds. The fragrant aroma of saltwater-filled air teased my nostrils. A trail of dust chased after a light silver Crown Victoria as it sped along the road toward the house. After pulling to a stop in the driveway, Laura Winters stepped out and ran a hand over her meticulously kept silver hair. Her husband, Tom, slid out from behind the driver's seat and smoothed the blazer over his customary polo shirt. I backed away from the window and continued into the kitchen.

I knew it was only a matter of time before they visited. It was something I had always been expecting in the back of my mind.

The wooden steps groaned as Tom and Laura climbed up to the porch and rapped on the door. I could just make out their ambiguous shapes on the other side of the opaque glass in the solid oak door before I opened it.

"Pastor. Laura."

"Hi, Martin," Tom responded. "How are things going?"

"As good as can be expected. Why don't you come in?"

Tom extended his hand as he stepped through the open doorway. I glanced down hesitantly at the gesture before reaching out and grasping it, perhaps with a little too much force. Laura's lips pressed together in a tight smile as she stepped past me into the house. I closed the door behind them and led the way into the living room.

"Won't you sit down? Can I get you something to drink?"

Tom and Laura eased down on the couch before declining my offer.

"So what brings you all the way out here?"

"We wanted to see how Rebecca was doing," Tom said.

"Not too well, I'm afraid. I had to take her to the hospital yesterday."

"We heard about that. That's why we stopped by."

"What happened?" Laura chimed in.

"I was fixing breakfast and called back to let her know, but she didn't come out. When I went in to check on her I found her on our bedroom floor. She started coughing violently and had stomach pains."

"So what did the doctors find out? Is she going to be okay?"

I struggled for a moment before opening my mouth. I knew that the second I told them what happened that it would become even more real than it already seemed. It was a realism that I wasn't sure if I was ready, or even strong enough, to handle. After thinking exactly how to best word my response, I answered his question. "She has Stage IV ovarian cancer. It's spread to her liver and the fluid around her lungs."

Laura's stiff and usually proper posture suddenly failed and she sank deeper into the couch. My mouth clamped shut as I watched her deflate right in front of my eyes. Tom remained steadfast in his seat and leaned in toward me with his elbows resting on his knees.

"The first doctor did blood work, which led to the MRI and CT scan," I continued. "Then they decided to do exploratory surgery. That's when they discovered how far it had spread."

"What can be done?" Tom asked.

"We're looking at radiation therapy and a few other options, but chances are it won't help much."

"What do you mean?" Laura questioned.

"The doctor told me that she has six months, at most."

Laura's jaw dropped. An unnerving silence clouded the room. "Martin, I'm so sorry."

I responded with a slight nod. "So am I."

"Would it be okay to see her, or is she up for that?"

"She's still asleep and pretty out of it, so now's not really a good time."

Tom leaned even closer. "You know that if you ever need anything, all you have to do is ask. Everyone in the church will be keeping you and Rebecca in their prayers."

"Thank you, Pastor."

For a minute, no one spoke. Laura appeared to be in a state

of shock after hearing the news, but Tom just sat there stoically. I sat across from them, trying to forget.

Finally, Laura broke the awkward silence. "Is there anything that you need?"

"No, but thank you anyway."

"Well, if there is, just let me know."

"I'll do that," I responded as I rose to my feet. "Thanks for stopping by. I really appreciate it. But Rebecca's sister came down yesterday, so she'll be here to help out for a while."

Nodding, Tom took Laura's hand and helped her up from the couch. They both followed me toward the foyer. I opened the door, making way for their exit. Laura walked out and, taking the handrail, eased down the steps. Tom stepped through the doorway but stopped and turned back to face me.

"One more thing, before we leave. Remember that all things work together for good to them that love God. Even though we can't understand why this is happening to Rebecca, we just trust Him."

I dropped my head before responding. "I know, I really do. It's just hard to do that right now—to trust Him."

"It usually is," Tom agreed. "But if you ever want to talk, you know how to reach me."

"Thanks, Pastor," I acknowledged, before abruptly closing the door. Hiding in the shadows behind the door, I leaned back against it and closed my eyes.

How can You take away the person that I love most in this world? And how can this be for my good? I screamed the words within my own mind. *I will never understand that. And I'll never forgive you for it.*

I raised my fist, wanting so badly to pound it against the door and yell at the top of my lungs. Why was this happening to me? I never did anything wrong. I was in church nearly every time the doors were open. I gave money in the offering plate on a regular basis. All of these things should count for something. And now the pastor had the nerve to tell me—in my own house—that this will all work out for good. The nerve of that man, walking in here acting like he knew everything that was going on. I didn't even have a clue what's going on, so what made him think he did?

The overwhelming sensation to hit something worked its way back through my bones. The wall beside the door looked like an incredibly tempting target. My fist would have punched through the thin drywall with relative ease, but asserting every ounce of self-control, I resisted the urge. The consequences of my would-be actions ran through my head. My fist began to relax, turning from a pale white to a soft pink as the blood flowed back through my veins. I walked out of the foyer and made my way toward the kitchen to brew a pot of fresh coffee. With any luck, that would suffice in calming my nerves.

* * *

I stepped into the bedroom with a tray carrying two cups of coffee and a plate of fresh fruit. Rebecca stirred and rolled over, looking up at me as I entered the room. I set the tray down on the table and bent down to give her a tender kiss.

"Good morning, honey."

"Morning. Who were you talking to?"

"When?"

"A few minutes ago," she replied, staring at me with the look she used when she wanted more answer than I offered.

"Oh, just Pastor Winters and Laura."

Rebecca tried to sit up, but only managed to slide up a few inches. "Are they still here?" she asked, craning her head to peer out into the hallway.

"No, they left a few minutes ago." I picked up the tray from the table and placed it in her lap. "Here, I want you to try to eat something."

"I'm not really hungry."

"I know, but still just try to eat a little." I kissed Rebecca on the cheek then stood up and meandered out of the room. "I'll be right back." As I paused in the doorway, Rebecca struggled to pull herself up a little higher and picked through the food on the plate.

I stepped out into the hallway, feeling lost, and stopped in the middle of the hall. The door to the studio called out to me again, beckoning me to reach for the knob and enter, but I resisted the urge and just stared at the closed door. I could hear the voice of the unfinished portrait sitting on the easel on the other side of the door. It was as clear as it was the night before. "Come finish me, Martin." The voice kept growing louder in my mind. Unable to withstand the calling, I inched forward. My hand grasped the door knob and twisted the cool metal handle. The soft clicking of the metal spring inside the knob echoed through the hall, ringing loudly in my ears. A sudden fit of coughing spilling from the bedroom snapped me out of the trance that the studio held over me. I backed away from the door and checked on Rebecca before retreating back down the hall toward the living room.

After giving Rebecca enough time to eat, I went to the bedroom to retrieve the tray and found her asleep. Most of the food remained uneaten. I leaned over and pressed my lips to her forehead. My lips lingered against her skin for several seconds before I pulled away. I remained standing over her, just looking down, before grabbing the tray and walking out of the room. As I got to the kitchen, the front door opened and Kelly walked into the house wearing a track suit and windbreaker. Even from across the room, I heard her heavy breathing as she draped her jacket over the back of the chair closest to the door.

"How was your run?"

"It was really good," she answered as she followed me into the kitchen. "I usually try to run at least two miles a day at home."

"That's a good goal to have. I would do the same thing except I lose track of time whenever I'm out on the beach."

Kelly glanced at the clock on the wall and her eyes grew a little wider. "Apparently it doesn't affect just you, since I was running for over an hour. There's something different about running here. It's much more relaxing."

"That's the effect this place has on you. That's probably why we love it here so much."

"I can see why, though I think I've always known," she trailed off as her attention drifted out the window toward the beach. "If it wasn't for Mark's job, I would have talked him into moving down here a long time ago."

"That would have been nice having you and the kids closer. But I don't think there's a big market for business law here." I poured another cup of coffee and sat down at the table.

Kelly poured herself a glass of water then turned from the window and leaned on the counter. "Yeah, I didn't think there would be. Though there is always Charleston."

We spent the next few minutes in silence. I sat at the table drinking my coffee while Kelly leaned against the counter taking an occasional sip from her glass of water. When I finished the coffee, I pushed myself away from the table and leaned past Kelly to place my cup in the sink then made for the door.

"How is she doing today?"

Her voice rang out through the silence. I stopped at the doorway, frozen in my tracks, and remained there for a few seconds before turning around to face her. "She seemed to be doing okay. Well, as much as can be expected. I got her to eat a little breakfast before she fell back asleep."

"Oh, okay," she responded. "I was going to go in and talk to her, but if she's sleeping, I wouldn't want to wake her up."

"Well, I'll let you in on a little secret. I really don't think she would mind if you woke her up."

A small smile crossed over Kelly's lips. "I know, I know. Maybe I'll just sit with her and read while she sleeps."

Smiling back at her, I stepped into the living room and fell onto the couch. Kelly followed me out and made a beeline straight for the bedroom. I watched her stop outside of the closed door. She raised her hand to knock on the door but froze. Easing the door open, she looked inside before slipping through the door and disappearing beyond the doorframe.

The toll of the past few days had taken an effect on me in ways I couldn't have possibly imagined. Though it was not even noon yet and I had only been up for a couple hours—a far cry from my usual six o'clock wake up call—a sudden rush of exhaustion devoured my body. I slouched down on the couch and allowed my head to fall back. My eyes remained fixated, staring at the ceiling until darkness washed over me.

I don't know how long I was asleep. The last thing I remembered was staring at the ceiling, counting the rotations of the fan. Then my eyes eased open and blinked away the remainder of my fatigue and tiredness. Kelly leaned over the couch, her hand shaking my shoulder.

"Wake up, sleepyhead." Her voice soothed my ears as I

fought my way back to complete consciousness.

"Oh, hey," I mumbled. "How long was I asleep?"

Kelly looked behind her at the clock on the wall. "Um, it's almost noon. I was back with Rebecca for about an hour or so."

"Man, I just felt really tired all of a sudden. I only meant to lay my head back and relax, but I must have been out the second my head hit the couch."

"Must have." She nodded back toward the bedroom. "Her throat was getting a little dry, so I came out to get her a drink. I thought about making lunch. Do you want anything while I'm in there?"

"You know you don't have to be fixing meals all the time. You may be family, but you're still a guest here."

"I know. I do it because I want to," Kelly responded, ruffling my hair. "And because I'm here to help out with whatever I can."

I was unable to successfully express my heartfelt appreciation for what Kelly was doing. Not many people would be so willing to leave their own family, especially with young children, to help out in a situation like this, even if it was for their own sister. In my opinion, Kelly was the true physical embodiment of an angel. Now if only her angelic status came with a miracle, I thought to myself as Kelly backed away from the couch and walked into the kitchen.

"Hey, I have an idea," I called out to her in the kitchen. "How about we order out instead of cooking tonight?"

"Anything in particular?"

"Well, there's an excellent Chinese place called New Dragon over in Hollywood." I paused. "It's really good, though we haven't had it in at least a month, I think," I tried to recall. It had definitely been a while since we ate Chinese. "I was thinking that some chicken and rice soup would be perfect for Bec, and I am craving sushi and Shrimp Chow Mai Fun."

"Sushi sounds great. Do you have a menu around here?"

"Yeah, should be on the fridge…no, wait, it's in the drawer under the microwave." I gave her a few seconds to rummage around the menus in the drawer. "Find it?"

"Got it, thanks. I don't know why I'm looking at it now though, since it's only lunch time. I need to take care of that first, don't you think?"

"That would probably be a good idea." I leaned forward, gathering the strength to get up from the couch. "Hey, do you want any help?"

"No, I got it, but thanks anyway."

I retrieved my book from the coffee table, flipped it open to my spot, and continued reading where I left off the other day, but had barely read four pages into the next section when Kelly walked out of the kitchen and held a plate over my shoulder. Dropping the book upside-down on the couch, I reached up and took the plate from her. On the plate was a corned beef sandwich with a handful of potato chips. It was even topped off with a huge, crunchy dill pickle on the side.

"Thanks." The aroma of the corned beef filled my nostrils. I could just make out the pungent scent of spicy brown mustard. With a quick "You're welcome" and a smile, Kelly returned to the kitchen and a moment later emerged holding a tray with a bowl of soup. She carried the tray back to the bedroom and disappeared through the doorway. I sat on the couch eating my lunch and getting lost in the therapeutic pages of my book.

"I take it that's a good book?" she asked.

Pulling myself from the page, I turned to look at her. "Oh

yeah, it's really good." My eyebrows curved upward. "How long have you been sitting there?"

"Probably about five minutes. You were so involved in the book that I didn't want to disturb you. What is it anyway?"

Shocked by my lack of awareness, it took a few seconds for her question to sink in. "Oh, it's the *Tao Te Ching*, by Lao Tzu."

"I've heard of Tzu but not that book. What's it about?"

"It's basically a collection of Chinese spiritual teachings, folk wisdom, cosmology, anti-Confucian doctrine, and mystical insights. It's also translated verbatim to allow a complete range of possible interpretations. Let's see what the cover says. 'The philosophy of Lao Tzu is simple: Accept what is in front of you without wanting the situation to be other than it is. Study the natural order of things and work with it rather than against it, for to try to change what is only sets up resistance. Nature provides everything without requiring payment or thanks, and also provides for all without discrimination - therefore let us present the same face to everyone and treat all men as equals, however they may behave. If we watch carefully, we will see that work proceeds more quickly and easily if we stop 'trying,' if we stop putting in so much extra effort, if we stop looking for results. In the clarity of a still and open mind, truth will be reflected. We will come to appreciate the original meaning of the word 'understand,' which means 'to stand under.' We serve whatever, or whoever, stands before us, without any thought for ourselves. Te, which may be translated as 'virtue' or 'strength,' lies always in Tao, or 'natural law.' In other words: Simply be.' "

My voice trailed off after reading the last few words. I had never really thought about the meaning of the book before. I'd spent the time reading it for entertainment and relaxation, never looking for a hidden, or deeper, meaning beyond that. But his philosophy of accepting what was in front of you without trying to change it brought a new meaning to my own situation. I glanced over at Kelly. She stared back at me with the same confused, but enlightened, look that I was giving her.

"Wow, that's really weird," I muttered. "I never put the pieces together like that before."

"It's strange how things work out like that but yet somehow refreshing."

"It is, isn't it?" My eyes drifted down to the book, somehow drawn to the cover art. I remained fixated on the black and white image on the cover. It was like a psychologist's test where you viewed a picture and explained what you saw, despite the fact that what you saw was nothing but a trick of the imagination. First, I saw a road through the mountains on the edge of a high cliff. Then I saw a single, black tree standing majestically at the top of the cover, its branches filling up the top portion of the frame. It suddenly occurred to me that even the cover illustrated the general principle of the book. Take things as they were, don't look for too much and don't over-analyze. Accept what was in front of you exactly as it was—what was there, nothing more, nothing less.

As the words of the book continued sinking in, I realized that the couch was not the place I needed to be. Marking the page, I closed the book, set it back on the coffee table, and excused myself from Kelly. I found Rebecca curled up in bed under the sheets. She stirred and looked up at me as I entered the room. Neither of us said a word as I curled up next to her and wrapped my arms around her body. I opened my mouth, but no words came out. It took a few minutes to speak, but once I did, the floodgates opened. We spent the next couple of hours curled up together talking about our fears and our life, everything and nothing at the same time.

With complete disregard for time, Rebecca and I remained in bed, talking. We were completely entranced in each other, our eyes unable to stray away from the other. A quiet knock on the door finally broke the spell. I opened the door and beckoned Kelly to come in.

"Hey, sorry to interrupt, but when did you want me to call the order in?"

My eyes locked on the clock next to the bed. It was almost five. "Oh, I didn't know it was so late."

"No, it's fine," Kelly replied. "It's not a problem. I just didn't know when you wanted to eat."

"You can call as soon as you've decided what you want. Do you need me to come out there and write down the order?"

"No, I remember it."

"Wait, what exactly are we planning?" Rebecca jumped in.

"We talked about ordering from New Dragon," I answered. "I was suddenly craving sushi and Shrimp Chow Mai Fun."

"Were you going to ask what I wanted?"

My focus drifted from Rebecca to Kelly and back to Rebecca before answering. "Well, I had thought to order you chicken and rice soup. I figured that would be good for your stomach."

"Maybe so, but I still might want something else," Rebecca retorted.

"I'm sorry, honey. What do you want?"

"A small bowl of chicken and rice soup would be good."

I just stared at her, dumbfounded, though I shouldn't have expected anything less from her after so many years. "All that for what I was going to get you in the first place?"

"Of course, I just wanted to be asked," she smiled over at me and leaned up to kiss my cheek. "Although, I could go for a small order of shrimp and broccoli."

Smiling as I shook my head, I raised my hands in concession. "As you wish, dear," I whispered, and then I looked up at Kelly still standing in the doorway.

"I got it. I'll call the order in once I figure out what I want. You kids have fun." As quickly as she appeared, Kelly disappeared through the doorway, closing the door behind her. She came back to tell us that the food would arrive in about thirty minutes.

Rebecca and I continued our 'everything and nothing' conversation while still lying in bed. It felt like no time had passed at all when I heard the doorbell ring. Through the closed door, I heard muffled speaking then the sound of footsteps approaching through the hallway. After a quick knock, Kelly poked her head into the bedroom and told us that the food had arrived and there was a surprise waiting for us as well. I jumped out of bed and helped Rebecca to her feet.

Chapter Eight

Still dressed in her pajamas, Rebecca grabbed a robe from the chair and threw it on before following me out of the bedroom. Rebecca and I froze as we stepped into the living room and found Leslie waiting.

"Leslie, hey," Rebecca stammered. "This is a nice surprise."

"It's funny how things work out. I was hanging out with some friends in Charleston and stopped at New Dragon to grab some food on my way home. I figured I would try it out since you and Martin always talked about how good it is. Anyway, I was there when your order was called in, so I thought I would just bring it over and join you, if that's okay."

"Sure, that's fine," I spoke up. "We'd love to have you join us."

"Great!" Leslie exclaimed. "This almost didn't work out. It took me a while to convince the guy at the counter that I really was going to bring your food to you. It was just lucky that one of the women who works there had been in the shop before and recognized me. So she vouched for me, even though the one guy still wasn't happy about it. So here I am."

"And here you are," I echoed back, my thought trailing off. Throughout the past year, both Rebecca and I had thought of Leslie as the child we had never had. It was a strange, yet refreshing, sight to see her in regular clothes instead of the usual tan khakis and green polo shirt. Her hair hung freely a couple of inches past her shoulders, instead of pulled back in her customary ponytail. There was the slightest hint of strategically placed curls. The way she wore her hair reminded me of Rebecca when we were in school.

Rebecca elbowed me in the ribs when she caught me staring at Leslie and smiling. "What's going on in that head of yours?" she whispered, leaning in closer.

"Just thinking about you," I answered with a grin and leaned in to kiss her. "You should know by now that it's a 24/7 Rebecca show inside of my head."

We followed Leslie and Kelly into the kitchen and joined them at the table where Kelly said the blessing. Leslie was at an obvious loss for words once we started eating. It had only been a day since returning from the hospital, but by now the whole community had to know about Rebecca. Despite the fact that Edisto Beach was a popular tourist area, the local, year-round community was a tight-knit group of people. And while I thought about Rebecca's illness, I made sure, as did everyone else at the table, not to bring the topic up in conversation.

After eating, we left the empty dishes on the table and retreated into the living room. The atmosphere was not as tense as it had been at the table. Rebecca and I cuddled up on the couch. Leslie sat on the loveseat, and Kelly was in the recliner. Rebecca made the mistake of asking Leslie how the shop was running, which launched into a twenty-five minute talk of the sales summary of the past few days, though I think Rebecca did it on purpose. She was absorbed in the conversation, throwing out comments and telling Leslie what a great job she was doing. I thought I even saw Rebecca smile several times during the discussion. The sight of that alone made my heart flutter and brought a smile to my face to match hers.

I glanced at the clock and was shocked to see that it was nearly ten. Three hours of conversation had passed without any of us realizing it. The others must have noticed me checking the time because they trailed off from talking and looked at the clock, or their own watches, as well. Leslie was the first to mention anything.

"Well, I guess I should be heading back," she said as she rose to her feet. "It was really fun."

"We'll have to do it again, soon," Rebecca said, and I nodded in agreement. "You are always welcome whenever you want, but you already knew that."

Leslie walked to the couch and leaned down to hug Rebecca. "I know. Thank you." She leaned toward me and offered another hug. "And you get one, too. I'll try to stop by after work on Saturday, if that's okay."

"Oh, that's fine," Rebecca answered. "But you don't have to make the drive up here that much. It is kind of far for you."

"No, I don't mind at all. I love coming up here." Leslie smiled at both of us then turned to Kelly. "It was really nice meeting you. I'm sure I'll see you again."

"Nice meeting you, too. And I'll be around for a while, so I'm sure we will see each other."

Leslie smiled back at the three of us one last time before grabbing her jacket from the chair and slipping it on. She paused at the front door long enough to wave goodbye then disappeared out into the night. Not long after Leslie's departure, Kelly excused herself and went into the kitchen to clean up, loading the dirty dishes in the dishwasher. Moments later she stepped back into the living room, stopping behind the couch.

"I'm going to call Mark and the kids before I go to bed. Do either of you need anything?"

I looked over at Rebecca then back up at Kelly. "No, we're good, thanks."

"Goodnight, hon," Rebecca said to her.

"Night, baby," Kelly responded and then disappeared down the hall toward her room.

Rebecca and I remained on the couch for a few minutes, her body curled up against mine. We stared out of the window into the blackness of the night. The location of the house so close to the water and the lack of outside street lights gave the most natural and pristine nighttime views. I contemplated asking if she wanted to sit on the porch swing for a bit but eventually decided against it. Instead, we enjoyed the view from the couch for a while before heading back to the bedroom. Before long, Rebecca and I were curled up in bed, her head resting on my chest and my arm around her shoulders, holding her close. Rebecca raised her head and kissed me before leaning over to flip off the lamp on the table. Her hand lingered on the switch for a second, hovering over the table.

"How tired are you?" she asked, without turning toward me.

"Not so much. Why?"

"Do you want to read to me?"

"Sure, I can do that. What is it that you're reading?" Rebecca retrieved *The Complete Poems of Emily Dickinson* from the table and handed it to me. "Ah, I should have known." I flipped open to her bookmark and began reading aloud.

I HAVE no life but this,
To lead it here;
Nor any death, but lest
Dispelled from there;
Nor tie to earths to come,
Nor action new,
Except through this extent,
The realm of you.

I read the last line and slammed the book shut, just managing to mark the page with my finger. Rebecca remained motionless with her head on my chest. Her eyes gazed off into space, fixed on an unseen point. "I'm sorry. I shouldn't have continued reading that."

"No, don't apologize," she responded, rubbing her hand along my chest. "I asked you to read to me in the first place, remember? I knew what the next few poems were about."

"I know, but still."

"It's fine, I promise. Please keep reading."

"Okay." I gave in, kissing her on the forehead before reading the next poem.

THE MOON is distant from the sea,
And yet with amber hands
She leads him, docile as a boy,
Along appointed sands.
He never misses a degree;
Obedient to her eye,
He comes just so far toward the town,
Just so far goes away.
Oh, Signor, thine the amber hand,
And mine the distant sea,—
Obedient to the least command
Thine eyes impose on me.

Rebecca nestled closer as I read several more poems. Even after she fell asleep, I kept reading in a whisper over her gentle, methodical breathing until my own eyes grew heavy. Moving as little as possible, I replaced the bookmark and left the book in its spot on the table. I reached for the lamp and flipped the switch. The room filled with a cool darkness as we lay there curled up in bed, arms intertwined around each other. Rebecca's rhythmic breathing lulled me into unconsciousness.

*   *   *

The next few days were a blur. I spent every moment of every day with Rebecca. Just being near her was intoxicating. I wanted nothing more than to be close to her, to touch her. Her fragrance overwhelmed my senses and I found myself lost in her aura. As the days passed, I became much quieter, giving into my worried thoughts. I had no clue what to say around my wife, but Rebecca somehow always knew what was going on inside my head.

Rebecca and I sat on the porch swing looking out over the rough Atlantic, just like we had done every morning since returning home from the hospital. The choppy waves broke ferociously against the shore without their typical rhythm. The unwritten and usually melodious symphony of the ocean was now random and out of tune. Intimidating grey clouds spanned across the distant horizon to the south of us. Rebecca leaned against me, wrapped up in a blanket, her head resting on my shoulder. There was a feeling in the air around us, as if something big was about to happen and everything knew it, the water, the sand, the air, the clouds. There was a storm brewing, literally and figuratively. I just wasn't exactly sure what it meant. But like so many times before, Rebecca knew something was bothering me and looked up at me with her piercing blue eyes. She didn't even have to speak; just the look she gave me was enough to make me want to pour my heart out.

"The water's really rough today, isn't it?"

"Yes, it is," I muttered, my eyes never leaving the horizon.

"I've always loved the ocean when it's like this. The way you can smell that a storm is coming, that change is coming. I love sitting out here when it's raining and just listening to the rain hit the roof, watching the tiny drops barrage the ocean."

"I do, too. It's so relaxing and peaceful. And the smell of the rain, I just can't describe it."

"Exactly, it's the perfect time to sit here and think, or contemplate things, or even just talk about whatever's on your mind, no matter how trivial it may be."

"That's assuming that there's something to talk, or think, about."

Rebecca leaned back a little and looked straight at me. "Are you saying there's not?"

"No," I responded without thinking. It took me a second to process her logic. "Wait, what?" I didn't know if it was her intention to do so, or it just happened naturally, but once again I found myself lost in a maddening state of confusion. Sometimes I think she did it on purpose, just to have fun.

She leaned in closer and whispered into my ear. "This is the point where you're supposed to tell me what's on your mind." Her warm breath hit my ear, sending shivers down my spine.

The tingling died down once her mouth moved away from my ear. I remained frozen in place until the final shiver escaped my body. "Am I really that transparent?"

"Yes, but only to me." She paused long enough for me to feign offense. "It's a gift, what can I say?"

"I'm not sure if I should take that as a compliment or not,"

I said, forcing a frown.

"Oh, you definitely should." She looked up at me before reaching up and running her fingers through my hair. "So tell me what's on your mind."

"I don't know, really. My mind is just a jumble of different things at the moment. There's so much going on that I really don't know where to start. I guess I'm a little apprehensive about the radiation therapy starting tomorrow."

"Shouldn't I be the one apprehensive about it?"

This was going all wrong. I was supposed to be cheering her up, not the other way around. "Well, yeah. It's just that…I don't know what it is. I guess I'm just worried."

Despite her strong front, one look into her eyes told me that she was just as worried as I was. I was relieved to know that I wasn't the only one feeling that way, but it did nothing to alleviate the anxiety. Not knowing what to say, all I could do was slip my arm around her shoulder and hold her body close to mine. The door opened behind us and Kelly stepped out onto the porch.

"Breakfast will be ready in a few minutes," she told us.

"Thanks. We'll be there in a second." The screen door banged against the frame as it slammed shut. "So I guess we should head inside, huh?" I pulled myself to my feet.

Rebecca stared out over the water, unmoving. "Yeah, but in a minute. Stay here with me. I want to keep talking."

I looked down at Rebecca. Her eyes gazed up at me, locked on my face and unwavering. Something in them told me that this was important. Without thinking twice, I sat back down and looped my arm around her shoulder.

Chapter Nine

Two seagulls rode into the strong updraft and appeared to float in place above the water. They broke off and dove straight down, skimmed a few feet above the choppy water, and snatched up a small fish in each powerful bill. The two birds soared back up towards the clouds with drops of sea-water trailing behind them.

"I would love to be a bird," Rebecca whispered, barely audible over the breeze blowing in from the water.

"What?"

"To be able to soar through the sky like that without a care in the world, it must feel so free, so amazing."

"I can only imagine."

"I've dreamt that I was a bird before. Did I ever tell you that?"

I looked over at her, still leaning up against me facing the water with her eyes closed, and kissed the side of her head. The sweet strawberry scent of her hair wafted up to my nostrils. My eyes closed as I inhaled a deep breath and wished this moment would last forever. I shook my head, but remembered her eyes were closed so she couldn't see me. "No, you didn't tell me."

"I would be soaring through the clouds, looking down on the world below. I wanted to stay up there forever, but somehow I always ended up back on the ground."

"Why's that?"

"It never failed. I would be flying over the house. When I saw it, I would dive down and fly past. You were always sitting on the porch, looking out over the water. After that, I wanted nothing more than to be back at home with you."

My eyes began to tear up the second the words left her mouth. A baseball-sized lump lodged in my throat. I looked toward the ceiling and blinked rapidly to keep myself from crying. When I got control over my emotions, I wrapped both arms around Rebecca and hugged her.

"I'm glad you always ended up coming back to me. I can't think of any other place in the world that I would want you to be other than here with me."

"And there is nowhere else I would rather be, either."

I pulled her closer and kissed her again. "Let's go eat," I whispered in her ear then helped her to her feet. The sound of the ocean faded as I closed the door behind us, but I knew that the moment we finished eating we would be back out on the porch, curled up together on the swing and listening to the waves crash along the shoreline. We always came back; or rather it was always the ocean that drew us back.

Just as I predicted, as soon as we finished lunch Rebecca and I hurried back to the swing and sat gazing out over the water. Even though the storm was still a couple hundred miles away, we could already see and feel the coming effects of it. Toward the southern horizon, the sky grew darker, almost pitch black. The wind was also building up. Every few minutes a strong gust blew across the front of the house. I was almost tempted to take Rebecca inside to spare her from the onslaught of the weather, but I knew she wouldn't pay any attention to my idea. So we sat in quiet contemplation, staring out over the vast expansiveness of the Atlantic.

Even rough and choppy, the ocean was still a beautiful sight to behold. Mesmerized by its fury, I couldn't believe it when Kelly came out and told us that it was after four in the afternoon. I helped Rebecca inside and left her on the couch with Kelly while I started fixing dinner. They read more poems from Rebecca's Emily Dickinson book while I cooked.

While I finished cleaning up after dinner, Kelly and Rebecca disappeared back into the bedroom. I emerged from the kitchen and collapsed onto the couch. After spending a few minutes just staring around the room, my eyes came to rest on my book on the coffee table. I again became engrossed in the writings of the *Tao Te Ching*, reading and rereading the passages to look for little gems hidden in the text.

"Rebecca's in bed, probably asleep by now," Kelly said when she sat down beside me hours later. "She was really tired."

"I wouldn't doubt it."

We sat there quietly for a moment before Kelly rose to her feet. "Well, I'll let you get back to your book. It's about time for me to make my daily phone call home."

She started to walk away and I felt the overwhelming urge to say something that I should have said so many times already. "Kelly, wait." I called out and looked up at her as she turned back toward me. "Thank you...for everything."

She smiled down at me, resting her hand on my shoulder.

"It's nothing that you wouldn't do for me."

I replaced my bookmark and set the book down on the coffee table. "Sit down and talk to me for a bit, unless you have to call Mark right now."

Kelly eased down next to me. Once again, we sat there in complete silence for a moment before I spoke up. "So how are you doing?"

"I'm okay, I guess. I'm dealing." She paused to look over at me. "I'm more concerned about how you two are doing."

"I'm learning to deal as well. Though, I am a little apprehensive about starting the radiation therapy tomorrow."

"You're not alone in that feeling."

I tilted my head and raised an eyebrow at her.

"I just meant that Rebecca is feeling the same way, at least that's what we were talking about a few minutes ago."

"I was wondering where you two disappeared to."

Except for a few sidelong glances at each other, we just sat there. The silence in the room screamed to be broken.

"I just don't know what to expect," I muttered. "I mean, she gets three radiation treatments a week, but how much will that really help? They already said she only has six months."

"I know, but we just have to keep thinking positive. I was reading through some literature at the hospital and it said that the survival rate of Stage IV ovarian cancer is twenty percent. So we shouldn't give up hope."

"It's just really hard not to, given all the circumstances."

Kelly reached over and squeezed my hand. Her show of comfort was better than any verbal response that she could have offered. After a few seconds, she released my hand and stood up. We exchanged quick goodnights and she walked back down the hall toward her bedroom. I reopened my book and resumed my reading.

*   *   *

We woke up early the next morning to get ready for our eleven o'clock appointment with the doctor. The therapy schedule was set up for Rebecca to receive treatment every Monday, Wednesday, and Friday over the next five weeks. At that time, the doctors would reevaluate her condition to see how she was progressing.

Every nerve ending in my body seemed to fire in unison as we drove to the hospital, but after the first few appointments the nervousness eventually died down. Rebecca seemed to be responding positively to the treatments. Everything seemed to be progressing just fine. She said she was feeling better, just not as strong due to the radiation and a little more tired than usual. When the five week treatment was up, they did more tests and discovered the tumors were shrinking slightly. Dr. Wallace gave Rebecca a week off before starting another five week treatment plan. The routine became second nature. Rebecca, Kelly, and I drove to the hospital, waited and paced, then drove back home.

The three of us sat in the living room after dinner on a rather warm Wednesday in late-November. After Rebecca's treatment earlier, we came home and spent the rest of the day relaxing. I told Kelly to take the afternoon off and go do something fun. She returned as I was finishing preparing dinner. Although she had already eaten, she joined us at the table and told us about her day as we ate. After dinner, we sat in the living room and talked until fatigue started to overtake Rebecca. We excused ourselves and I helped her back to the bedroom. I turned out the light and sat down in the chair next to her. The faint light shining in through the cracked door gave just enough illumination for me to be able to watch my wife as I did every night after she fell asleep. After almost an hour, I began to nod off and had just entered the first stages of sleep when Rebecca's voice pierced through the darkness.

"How long have you been sitting there?"

"The whole time," I replied, yawning. "Do you feel any better?"

"A little," she responded as she shifted in the bed, pulling herself up to a sitting position. "You don't have to stay right next to me all day. You know that, right?"

"I do, but I want to be here."

"I know, but I'm just saying that you don't have to be here and not do anything else. You've been by my side for almost three weeks straight."

"Where else would I be other than here with you?"

"Well, for starters, you could be painting," she retorted.

"I can't paint with everything that's going on."

Even through the darkened room, I felt Rebecca's eyes boring right through me. "What's the real reason?"

"I just told you," I responded. "There's just so much going on right now that I don't have the time to paint."

"Are you sure there's nothing more to it?"

She always found a way to draw out every last detail, whether I wanted to share it or not. So once again, I found myself spilling everything to her. "I just can't paint right now, not with you like you are. It just hurts to go in there and see your painting looking back at me."

"I want you to finish my portrait," she pleaded.

"Now?"

"Well, not right this minute. Not even tomorrow, or whenever, not if you can't, like you say. I just want you to promise me that you will finish it at some point."

She looked at me, and even through the partial darkness I could see deep into her eyes. There was something about them that just made me melt and give into anything and everything that she wanted. "I'll finish it. I promise."

"Thank you," she said. I heard the relief ringing in her voice. "Come lay with me."

I pushed myself out of the chair and climbed into bed with her. I wrapped both of my arms around her, pulling her into my body. Her fingers ran through my hair for a few minutes until she fell back asleep. I held her close and stared down at her in the dim light. A wave of emotion washed over me. My eyes welled up with tears. I pressed my lips to her forehead and lingered, just breathing her in, for what seemed like an eternity until sleep took another hold on me.

Somewhere outside a bird chirped, pulling me out of a light sleep. Faint traces of the mid-morning sun peeked through the curtains and cast a soft reddish glow over the room. I readjusted my position in the bed so I could wrap both arms around Rebecca without waking her and rested my head against hers. My eyes closed and I willed sleep to return. Faint footsteps slowly approached to the door. After a quiet knock, the door opened and Kelly poked her head in.

"Morning," she whispered from the doorway as Rebecca stirred in her sleep. "I was beginning to think that you two were planning to sleep the whole day."

I raised my head in an attempt to look at the clock. "What time is it?"

"Almost eleven."

"Are you kidding me?" I detangled myself from Rebecca and climbed out of bed. As I stepped into the bathroom to brush my teeth, Kelly crossed the room and sat down in the chair next to the bed. She took Rebecca's hand and began to caress it. After a few strokes, Rebecca's eyes opened and she squinted until her eyes adjusted to the light. I watched from the bathroom, noticing how her forehead crinkled up as she squinted and her nose scrunched up ever so slightly. I had noticed these little things many times before, but they didn't stand out in my mind like they did at that moment.

"Morning, sunshine. How are you feeling?"

Rebecca didn't respond, just shrugging her shoulders. I finished brushing my teeth and rinsed my mouth in the sink. Scurrying out of the bathroom, I leaned over the bed and kissed Rebecca on the forehead before heading out of the room. I paused halfway down the hall, then turned and headed back to the doorway.

"Do either of you want anything to eat?"

Rebecca shook her head and then rested it back on the pillow. Kelly turned in the chair to look at me. "No thanks, I already ate something earlier."

I backed out of the doorway and walked down the hall toward the kitchen. As I left, I heard Rebecca and Kelly talking, their voices fading the farther away I got. Once in the kitchen, I downed a bowl of cereal and sipped from a cup of coffee as I read over the headlines of the newspaper. The coffee ran out just as I started the final section of the paper. I refolded the paper and replaced it back on the other side of the table, then made my way to the sink with the dirty dishes.

"Martin!" Kelly yelled from the bedroom. "Get back here."

It was as if time stopped. The dishes slipped from my hand. They hung, frozen, in the air. The coffee mug caught the edge of the counter. Fragments of ceramic chips rained down. I rushed out of the kitchen. I froze when I stepped into the bedroom. Rebecca hung off of the edge of the bed. Her face buried in a trash can. Muffled sounds escaped from the opening. An agonizing, retching hacking. Kelly knelt on the floor next to the bed. Her one arm supported Rebecca. The other held the trash can.

A thousand thoughts flashed through my mind. I could only form a single coherent sentence. "What happened?"

"I don't know," Kelly responded. Her eyes never left Rebecca. "We were talking and then she just started throwing up."

I sprinted across the room in an instant. Flinging the chair aside, I collapsed onto the floor. My hands immediately moved to Rebecca. I held her hair with one as the other took the trash can from Kelly.

Once I was situated, Kelly stepped back and looked down at us with a horrified look on her face. "She just stopped in mid-sentence and started throwing up. Even after everything was out, she still kept going with dry heaves."

"This is supposed to be a reaction to the radiation, isn't it?"

"Yeah, but it didn't happen the first time and it's not supposed to go on for this long, is it?" Kelly countered.

"No, it's not supposed to keep going like this. If it doesn't stop in a minute, we need to get her to the hospital." I questioned everything we had read about radiation therapy the past few weeks.

"No argument from me," Kelly agreed, hovering over the two of us as Rebecca continued dry heaving into the trash can. "This has gone on long enough. We have to get her to the hospital." My eyes locked onto the dresser. Right on my keys. Kelly followed my gaze, saw the keys, and grabbed them.

"I'll get the car started."

Then Kelly was gone. I scooped Rebecca into my arms. Rebecca hooked one arm around my neck and clutched the trash can with the other. I darted out of the room. Kelly already had the car running when I crashed out the front door. I helped Rebecca in the back seat and fastened her seat belt. Kelly climbed in the back seat next to Rebecca. I slid behind the wheel, threw the car in gear, and raced down the street.

* * *

During the past two months, I had spent more time in the hospital than I would ever have wanted to spend in an entire lifetime. I had almost gotten used to the musty, druggy smell. Kelly paced the floor in front of me, her hand cupped around the back of her neck. She stopped pacing, but the sound of footsteps still rang out through the hall. I looked up to see Dr. Lankford walking toward us. I pulled myself to my feet to wait for the doctor. My legs barely supported the weight as I stood up. Kelly shuffled backward and ended up next to me, her arm looped through my own. Dr. Lankford stood in front of us, his lips pressed together. We held eye contact for a brief second before his chin dropped and he shook his head.

"I'm sorry, Mr. Banks. We lost her."

My entire body went numb as I collapsed back into the chair, pulling Kelly off balance as I fell. She managed to fall into the chair next to me. I looked up at Dr. Lankford with watery eyes and tried to formulate a response, a question, anything, but nothing came out of my mouth. Kelly put her arm around my shoulder, but I felt nothing, no contact, no feeling. It was as if all my senses had shut down. She rested her head on my shoulder and began crying. My eyes in turn opened and the warm tears started streaming down my cheeks through the coldness of the room.

Chapter Ten

It seemed that weather and funerals were somehow cosmically tied together. When my grandmother died twenty years earlier the skies let loose with a torrential downpour as we drove to the gravesite. The rain lasted all the way through the graveside ceremony. It was as if the weather knew that my grandmother had died and was grieving along with us. The same gloomy skies lurked overhead at both mine and Rebecca's parents' funerals. And today was no different.

Under dark and threatening clouds, I stared out over the cemetery.. Hundreds of similar looking headstones marked each individual plot. It didn't seem right that they all had the same exact marker above their final resting spot. Every single person buried here had been a separate person. They had their own life, their own family. Even my parents had individual headstones above their plots up in Wilmington. And now I was putting my wife in a plot where she didn't belong, where she would fade into all the other headstones. Why did everyone in my family seem to die before it was their time?

I was alone, not only in the figurative sense, but in the literal sense, as well. No one else was around yet. I had left the funeral home the second it was over to make my way to the gravesite, to be alone with my thoughts before everyone else arrived. Rebecca's tent-covered plot had been excavated, the mound of unearthed dirt covered by a tarp. A huge oak tree rose gallantly toward the sky not far from the site. Somehow, I found myself standing under its canopy of barren limbs, staring once again over the endless hills of white headstones. A small crowd slowly began to gather around the tent. When I looked over, Kelly was heading toward me. She looped her arm through mine and rested her head on my shoulder. We stood under the awning of branches in silence for a few moments before she said anything.

"We're ready to start whenever you are."

I looked down at her and then rested my cheek against the side of her head. "I'll be there in a second," I whispered.

With a gentle squeeze of my arm, Kelly stepped away and went back to the tent. I watched as she walked back to her own family. Mark and the kids had driven down from Greenville the day before and stopped by the house for dinner. Kelly had cooked a large meal, since they would all be there. I remained in a daze the entire time. A hurricane could have sliced through the island, ripping my house to shreds, and I probably wouldn't have noticed.

I pushed away from the tree trunk and walked toward the tent. Everyone seemed to quiet down as I approached. The majority of the men extended their hands to me as I passed by. I shook everyone's hand who offered so as not to be rude, but I just wished that the service would be over so I could be alone. The only thing I longed for at the moment was solitude.

Tom Winters stood at the head of the crowd, talking to Mark. Tom had offered to perform the ceremony for me when he stopped by the day after Rebecca died, and I agreed since it would be one less thing I had to think about. Laura sat off to the side in one of the few chairs that were set up beside the casket, right beside Leslie. I found my place next to Kelly and the kids across the casket from Laura. My hand drifted down to Kelly's shoulder. Her hand slid up to rest on mine. Mark came over and stood next to me as the service began. He persuaded me to take the seat next to Kelly. Not long after Tom's second sentence, my mind drifted into unconsciousness. I didn't want to hear anything that was being said. I didn't want to be around anyone who was here. I knew it would be a short service, but nowhere near short enough. The one thing on my mind was getting it over with so that I could get away from everything and everyone.

As if on cue, my mind snapped back to attention and I made my way toward Tom and stood beside him as he began winding down. I heard myself fumbling through a few words in closing. Afterward, I placed a rose on the casket and then Kelly and her family placed their roses to close out the service.

As everyone stood up and stepped out of the shelter of the tent, I went to the casket again and my fingers traced along the smooth maroon exterior. My hand drifted into the inside pocket of my suit and pulled out two folded-up pieces of paper. I unfolded the first piece, faded and yellow, a testament of the years. The handwritten words that I wrote so long ago had long since started to fade. My eyes scanned each line, reading in a whisper to myself as all other sound was blocked out. I mouthed the lines of the second page, scanning each of Rebecca's penned words before refolding the papers. Tears formed in my eyes as I raised both hands to my face and held each folded page to my lips. Both pieces slid snugly into the tight gap on the lid beneath the various roses. I turned and started to weave my way through the crowd toward my car as fast as I could manage.

"Martin," Pastor Winters called from behind me. "Wait a minute."

I turned to wait for him as he jogged toward me. He carried himself well for a man of nearly sixty-five. The strong breeze blew through his wispy gray hair as he drew nearer to me.

"Are you okay?" he asked during his final steps.

I'm sure that the look on my face was enough to answer his question, but just to be sure, I attempted to vocalize my expression. "Do you really have to ask that?"

"I'm sorry. I know this probably isn't the right time, but is there anything I can do for you?"

It took all of my self-control not to give a sarcastic answer. "Not unless you can turn the clock back and make it so Bec is still alive."

Tom just looked back at me with an air of complete understanding. He had probably heard similar sentiments before. "You know that's not possible."

"Then there's nothing you can do."

My quick response brought an onset of silence that held until Kelly approached with Sean in tow. When the boy spied me, he pulled away and somehow managed to wiggle free from her grasp. He sprinted headlong toward me and lunged through the air. His arms wrapped around my leg and clutched on for dear life. I knelt down to let him latch around my neck then I took him in my arms and stood up. We slowly backed away from Pastor Winters and Kelly as Sean watched a squirrel scamper across the grass toward a tree. He pointed at the tree and we meandered in its general direction. I overheard Kelly offer an explanation for my behavior as I walked away.

"This is really hard for him."

"I know," Pastor Winters responded. "But it's hard for me to sit back and not help when someone is in obvious pain like that."

"I can relate. It's just going to take him some time before he'll let anyone try to help."

As I looked back at them, Pastor Winters stared straight at me as if his comment was for me to hear instead of Kelly. "As long as he knows that I'll be here to help him when he wants help."

"He does," she told him. "It's just going to take some time."

I felt the warmth pulsating through my cheeks as the anger built up inside. They were talking about me as if I weren't standing a mere twenty feet away. Granted I wasn't actually a part of the conversation, but I still heard every word they said. What was so hard for them to understand? All I wanted was to just be left alone.

"What about you?" Pastor Winters asked. "Are you okay?"

Mark and their other two kids, Jesse and Cheryl, walked up and stopped beside Kelly and Pastor Winters. Kelly paused to look back at her husband before answering.

"I will be," she said, smiling at Mark. "They'll help me through it."

"How long are you going to be around?"

"I'm not really sure. Probably a couple more days."

Pastor Winters drew his gaze away from me. "Good, at least Martin doesn't have to be alone the whole time."

"For a couple days, at least," Kelly agreed.

Furious, I hurried back to the group and passed Sean over to Kelly. "I'm heading back home."

"If there's anything I can do, just let me know." A forced smile spread over the pastor's face which only served to enrage me further. He extended his hand.

"I'll do that," I snapped over my shoulder as I hurried toward my car.

As I escaped from earshot, I barely overheard Mark commenting to Pastor Winters about how beautiful the service was. I climbed behind the wheel of the car and stared down at the gauges. After pausing for a few seconds to calm myself down, I slid the key into the ignition and started the car. As I pulled away, Kelly waved as she, Mark, and the kids walked toward their car. My attention drifted back to the road as I drove home.

My focus faded in and out during the drive home from the cemetery. Somehow I managed to make it home without running off of the road or hitting someone. I pulled into the driveway and slid out of the car, pausing for a second to look out over the rough, choppy water. The ocean always commanded my complete attention. Some aspect of the water always seemed to soothe me, no matter how rough it was.

I climbed the steps and walked into the house. The second I stepped through the door, I met face to face with a coldness and emptiness. All I could think of was to get back to the water. The world around me turned to a blur as I hurried back to the porch, stopping in front of the swing overlooking the water. Through the open front door, I heard the phone ring. I ignored the shrill tone and sat down on the swing, allowing my mind to drift off as I stared out over the water. An invisible curtain fell over my vision while I sat lost in my thoughts. The peacefulness of the scene, along with the constant crashing of the waves, lulled me from consciousness. My eyes fell shut and only the rhythmic crashing of the waves permeated my mind.

The blackness faded into a blur that materialized into the beach below me. I looked around and shook my head to regain my bearings. The front door opened behind me with a long, drawn-out squeak of the hinges. I made a mental note to oil the hinges as I twisted around expecting to see Kelly. My heart stopped. Standing behind me in the doorway was not Kelly, but Rebecca. She smiled at me as she walked toward the swing. Instinctively, I closed my eyes and shook my head. I opened them again and looked up at the apparition standing above me. It was still Rebecca. She sat down on the swing next to me and kissed my cheek before resting her head on my shoulder. I sat, frozen, as I stared down at her.

"Bec?"

She raised her head to look up at me, her wide blue eyes burning into mine. "Yes?"

"Wh-what's going on here?"

"What do you mean?"

"You're here...with me."

She stared up at me. "Sorry, I'm a little lost. What's the problem with that?"

"The problem is you shouldn't be here," I pushed myself up from the swing and paced back and forth on the porch. "This is a dream. It has to be a dream."

"Well, where else would I be?" Rebecca questioned as she watched me pace.

"Well, first of all, not here," I answered, stopping to lean on the railing with my back to the calm water. "Considering I just came from your funeral."

Rebecca sat up straight and turned to face me. "What are you talking about? How could I possibly be here if you just came from my funeral?"

"I don't know. That's exactly what I was just asking myself." The rhythmic pounding of the waves on the shoreline fought to silence my own thoughts. Unable to process the information inside my head, my brain went into sensory overload. "I don't understand what's going on here." I continued pacing back and forth on the porch. "It has to be a dream. That's the only logical explanation."

Rebecca stood up and looped her arm through mine. "Why does this have to be the dream?"

I looked down at her arm nuzzled against mine. It felt real enough, but it couldn't be. Could it? How could this be real? I turned toward Rebecca and searched her eyes. Every single fiber of my body wanted to believe that this was reality. "If only that were the truth."

"But truth is what we make it out to be, isn't it? The same can be said for reality."

"If it were only that simple." I took both of her hands in mine. "Believe me, there is nothing more I could ever want than to have you here with me."

"I'm sensing that there's a 'but' coming." Rebecca eased herself down on the swing and swayed back and forth.

I eased down next to her and slipped one arm around her shoulders. "You're right. There is a 'but,' but I'm not really sure what it is yet."

"Well, do you want to try to talk about it? Maybe that will help you to sort things out. I mean, it's worth a shot, isn't it?"

"Normally, I would jump at the chance to sit and talk to

you, but there's just one problem with that." I paused for a second to gather my words. "The problem is that you're not really here. You're not real. Nothing I talk about would matter, because we can't change any of it."

Rebecca pulled away. She stood up and leaned on the railing. "How can you say that? I'm standing right here in front of you."

"Well, believe me, when I figure out how that's possible, you'll be the first to know."

"Why does it have to be like that? It can't be that hard to accept that I am right here in front of you. Reality is all in the mind of the beholder. It's all in how the brain interprets things."

"It's not that simple anymore."

"Why are you acting like this?" Rebecca turned away from me, looking out over the suddenly tumultuous water. "I just don't understand."

I lurched to my feet, sending the swing bouncing recklessly on its chain. "You don't understand because you're dead. Dead people can't understand anything."

"I don't have to take this from you," Rebecca cried as she ran toward the door. "I didn't do anything."

"You didn't do anything?" I called out, my voice rising louder. "How exactly do you figure that?"

"I'm not doing this with you right now. I'm leaving."

"Go right ahead. You do that."

Rebecca froze at the door with her hand on the knob. Her head snapped toward me. I turned away and leaned over the railing. My eyes remained locked on the choppy waves.

"And what exactly is that supposed to mean?"

"Exactly what I said, you're the one who left me here all

alone."

"Oh, so let's say that for the sake of argument, I'm dead. Apparently I'm responsible for my own death? I wasn't aware that was something I could control."

"Yeah, well, it doesn't change the fact that you left me here. You were supposed to have six months. Six months! It wasn't even two months and you were gone."

Rebecca's jaw dropped as she stared at me through glistening eyes. My stomach tightened in knots. I turned away for a second, but when I turned back, the porch was empty. "Bec, I'm sorry," I called out as I rushed toward the door. "I didn't mean it."

I flung open the door and ran through the house, calling out for Rebecca, but she was nowhere to be found. I returned to the porch and stood there by the swing. I prayed that she would walk back out of the door as suddenly as she had appeared a few minutes earlier.

It never happened. She never came back. I remained alone on the porch. The sequence replayed over and over in my head. I tried to justify my actions by convincing myself it was a dream. If Rebecca had really been there, I would have never treated her like that, no matter what. I fell back on the swing, the chains buckling under the sudden weight of my collapse. My head weighed down heavily on my shoulders. Deep within the pit of my stomach, the restless feeling grew stronger. As I buried my face in my hands, I felt sick to my stomach.

Chapter Eleven

A car sped down the road toward the house, leaving a billowing cloud of dust in its wake. Nearing the house, the car slowed down and pulled into the driveway. Kelly slipped out from behind the wheel and walked toward the steps. She stopped behind the swing and looked down at me as I went back to staring out over the water.

"Hey, I tried to call you a little while ago," she said.

Her words went in one ear and spilled right out of the other. I remained a human statue, my attention fixated somewhere over the curling whitecaps.

"I was hoping you'd just come back here," she continued. "I wanted to make sure you were okay."

She stepped around the swing and sat down next to me. The rhythmic swaying of the swing buckled as she sat down. I glanced over at her but still said nothing.

"I would have been here sooner, but I went with Mark and the kids back to the hotel for a bit."

I finally pried my eyes away from the foaming water and

turned toward her. "How are they doing?"

"They're okay, for the most part. Sean doesn't really understand what all of this means, so he was asking a lot of questions as we left."

"Well, he's a smart kid, but still, just a kid."

Kelly took in a long breath before continuing. "And I wanted to see how you were doing. You left the cemetery so abruptly."

The image flashed through my mind. I felt myself getting flustered as the emotions started to build up again. I took a few deep, calming breaths to regain my composure and nodded. "I wasn't exactly in the mood to stick around, not with everyone standing there talking about me."

"It's just because they care about you."

"I know, but still. They could have had the decency to do it after I left, you know?"

The two of us sat in silence. My eyes were once again shrouded by an invisible curtain as I sat lost in my own thoughts. All I could see was the water in front of me. Everything else faded into nothing.

Kelly stood up and walked around behind the swing, stopping to rest her hand on my shoulder. "Yeah, well…I'll just let you be alone for a little while," she said and then walked toward the door.

I fought the battle between speaking and remaining silent. I wanted to tell her what had happened, but a part of me just wanted to believe it had never actually happened. I wrestled with myself as Kelly opened the front door.

"I got in a fight with Rebecca."

Kelly paused for a brief second before she crossed the porch and eased back down on the swing next to me. "When was that? She never told me anything."

Looking straight ahead at the water, my gaze never faltered as I whispered my response. "About ten minutes ago."

"What-what exactly do you mean by that?"

"I'm not exactly sure what happened," I trailed off as I tried to figure out what to say. "I got home and was sitting out here, then the next thing I knew Bec came out of the house and sat down next to me as if nothing had happened. I kept telling myself it was a dream and not actually real." I looked over at her. "But that doesn't excuse what I did. I completely lost it."

"What did you do?"

"I flipped out and yelled at her for leaving. And what's worse is that I blamed her for dying. I blamed it on her."

Kelly's eyes opened wide. The several deep inhalations she took resounded over the crashing waves below us. She pushed herself to her feet and leaned on the railing. "I'm not going to say it was the best thing to do, but it's not unexpected. You just lost someone very important to you. It's natural to be angry and hurt about that."

"I know," I replied. "But I shouldn't be angry at Bec. She wasn't the one in control of it all."

"Then who do you blame? The doctors?"

"Not really. I know they did all they could do. Though I still don't understand how they couldn't pick up on the cancer sooner. But no, I don't blame them. They aren't in control either."

"So you're blaming God for it? Is that what you're getting at?"

"If the shoe fits…"

Kelly sat back down and paused for a moment to look out over the water. "Let me ask one thing. What good will that do?"

"Probably none, but it does make me feel better. It's something, or rather somebody, that I can focus my anger on."

Kelly slipped her arm around my shoulder and leaned in closer to me. "I'm going to tell you something that I tell my kids. Being mad about the past does nothing to change the future. It will only eat you up inside and keep you from being happy."

"What could I possibly have to be happy about?" I retorted.

"Look, I know you're going through a rough time right now and that you're hurting, but that doesn't mean you can just go around being rude to people who love you and care about you. You aren't the only one who is hurting right now."

I heard every word Kelly said, but I didn't acknowledge it. Instead, I just sat there and stared out over the water, willing for everything around me to just fade into nothing.

Kelly rose to her feet and looked down at me. "Well, I'll leave you alone for a while. If you happen to need anything, I'll be inside." The screen door banged shut as she disappeared into the house.

*   *   *

The setting sun disappeared over the horizon behind me, filling the breaks in the cloudy evening sky with a fiery intensity. Kelly walked out on the porch and sat down beside me. We exchanged greetings as she wrapped a blanket around me.

"It's getting chilly and you don't seem too interested in coming inside yet," she said. "So I figured this would keep you warm until you came in."

I glanced over at her and forced a smile. "Thank you."

"It's nothing," she responded as she rose to her feet.

I'm sorry, my mind screamed, though the words didn't

come out. I watched Kelly walk across the porch and knew that I had to stop her. "No, wait. Don't go."

Kelly stopped and looked back at me for a second before returning to the swing. My gaze shifted from the water down to the corner of the porch as I searched my soul for the right words to say.

"I'm sorry about earlier. I didn't mean to snap at you and I am definitely not mad at you. This is just really hard for me. But I've really appreciated everything you've done around here lately."

"And I'm sorry too. I shouldn't have tried to tell you how to feel or how to grieve. Everyone does it in their own way." She slipped her arm around me and rubbed my shoulder. "And I do know how hard this is for you. I'm feeling the same way about things. That makes me an excellent person to talk to, if you ever need it."

"I know, and I appreciate it. I'm just not sure I'm ready to talk about things yet."

"I figured as much," she nodded. "But the offer is always there if you ever need it." She pulled herself to her feet. "By the way, I left a plate of sandwiches for you covered in the refrigerator. So it's there whenever you want to eat."

"Okay, thanks," I replied out of habit, pausing for a second to look up at her.

Kelly stood over me for the longest time. It was then that I noticed that she was dressed as if she were about to go out, wearing a light jacket with her purse slung over one shoulder. Her hair was pulled back in a sloppy ponytail, but a few strands still hung down each side of her face.

"Were you about to leave?" I asked.

"Yeah, I was going to stop by the hotel and see Mark and

the kids for a while. They are going back home tomorrow and I wanted to see them before they left."

"So are you going to stay with them tonight or come back here?"

She leaned up against the railing. "I thought about staying but decided that wouldn't be a good idea. And I don't want to leave you here alone in the house tonight."

"I appreciate the thought, but you can stay there if you want. I don't mind. You've already done so much here and been away from your own family for so long."

"That's true," she agreed. "But just remember one thing. You're a part of my family, too. That's never going to change." She paused and looked back over the water. I tried to formulate a response, but nothing came out. "Well, I'll let you get back to thinking, or whatever," she continued. "I guess I'll see you tomorrow."

As if an afterthought as she walked down the steps, I called after her. "Tell Mark thanks for being here and bringing the kids up. And for not minding your being gone for so long."

"I'll do that," Kelly said over her shoulder.

I watched from the swing as she slid behind the wheel, started the car, and backed down the driveway. Once the tail-lights disappeared around the bend, my gaze returned to the ocean. I hated to admit it, but I was feeling a little better. I wasn't as angry as I had been earlier. It was just hard to explain exactly what I was feeling. Then the loud rumble of my stomach snapped me out of my thoughts. I walked inside to check the refrigerator and see what was left for dinner. Every shelf was packed full of plates, or trays, of food that families from the church had sent over the past few days.

*   *   *

That night gave me the first taste of my new life, a life without Rebecca. As I sat alone, I noticed how quiet the house was. An empty plate remained on the table in front of me, unmoved in the hour or so since I finished eating. The small light over the sink provided the only source of light in the dark house. Deafening silence filled the air, broken only by my rhythmic breathing. It was even unusually quiet outside of the house. The crashing of the rolling waves, the chirping of crickets, I could hear nothing at all. All the normal sounds had faded back into nothingness. I fought the feeling that this was how it would be from now on.

I pushed away from the table and rose to my feet then dropped my plate and cup into the sink and switched off the light. The room plunged into complete darkness. Even in the murky blackness, it was easy to find my way through the house. And it wasn't as if turning on the lights would help to warm the place up. There was something about darkness that was soothing, even calming. Maybe it was the way that it completely enveloped me, like a blanket surrounding me.

Somehow, I ended up in the bedroom, sitting in the chair next to the bed. Time grew irrelevant as I stared into the black void filling the room. The soft ticking of the wall clock hypnotized me as the hours passed with excruciating slowness.

A wandering ray of moonlight shone through a narrow slit in the curtain, cutting through the darkness and across my face. I pulled myself out of the hypnotic trance that had consumed me and glanced out of the window. The clouds pulled back to reveal the soft light of the crescent moon reflecting off of the rippling water. Every so often, the light strayed through the window into the bedroom and cast shimmering waves of shadows and light along the wall. I reached out for the curtains and pulled them closed to block out the plague of dancing light.

Pushing through the blinding darkness of the room, my hand found the doorknob. I stepped out into the hallway and walked blindly toward the living room. The clock on the VCR read ten after three as I pulled back the curtain and looked out the window. I left a small part in the curtain, allowing a faint stream of light to enter the room.

I usually never had problems sleeping through the night, or getting to sleep for that matter, but this was not like any other night in my life. I grabbed a jacket from the hall closet and slipped it on before reaching for the doorknob. It seemed that the quieter I tried to be, the more noise I made. The floorboards creaked and groaned with each step I took. As I eased open the front door, the metal of the hinges ground together and emitted a drawn-out, high-pitched squeal. I decided to abandon all cautiousness and just yanked the door open. Surprisingly, not a sound was made and the hinges stopped squeaking. Then it struck me. I didn't know why I felt the need to be quiet, since I was all alone in the house.

I stepped outside and closed the door behind me. The air was crisp and clear. The smell of salt and sand bombarded my nostrils. It was just cold enough that I could see the faint puffs of white as the warmth of my breath condensed in the chilled air under the moonlight. I leaned against the railing just beside the steps and looked up toward the crescent moon. Every so often the clouds slipped in front and hid the little sliver. I stared at the fleeting trails of breath left in the air around me. Eventually the clouds drifted past, unveiling the moon and allowing its soft light to illuminate the sky once again.

The salty air rejuvenated me and erased all traces of fatigue and tiredness as I walked down the steps. The grass crunched beneath my feet as I found myself heading toward the shore.

The moonlight shimmered off of the rippling water. I climbed up one of the small sand dunes and looked at the serene setting before continuing along the shoreline.

Chapter Twelve

Kelly returned to the house the next morning and passed by with nothing more than a smile on her way inside. She fixed a fresh pot of coffee and ventured back out onto the porch, bringing two steaming mugs. I sat staring out over the water as the waves rolled into the shore, sending up plumes of white spray. She stopped behind me and handed me one of the mugs. She leaned against the railing.

"Morning," she said. "How long have you been up?"

My gaze never faltered from the water as I offered a mumbled response. "Since about seven...yesterday morning."

Kelly's eyes locked onto me as her mouth hung open. "You didn't sleep at all last night?"

"I wasn't tired so I ended up going for a walk, then just sat out here and watched the sun rise."

Kelly sat down on the swing next to me, her body facing mine. "I want you to do me a favor." Her quiet voice echoed through the air. "I don't want you to get in the habit of doing things like this. I'd rather not have to worry about you all the time after I leave."

I looked over at her. Her brown eyes stared intently back at me, unwavering. The edges of my mouth curved upward in an attempted smile.

"I was about to go for my morning run," Kelly continued. "But I think I'll just stick around here instead."

"No, go. Run. Don't stay here on my account."

"I just don't want to leave you alone unless you're going to be okay."

"I'll be fine, don't worry about me." My eyes remained fixated on hers. "I promise. Now go."

Kelly raised her eyebrow at me before a smile crept across her face. She pushed herself up from the swing and went inside. A few minutes later, she came back out and waved to me as she bounced down the steps to begin her run. I remained on the swing long after she disappeared down the beach, staring off into nothingness. I stood up and walked inside to the living room.

I fell on the couch and propped my feet up on the coffee table as my head collapsed back. My gaze drifted up to the ceiling then around the room before it came to rest on the antique desk with an old worn yearbook sitting in the corner. I looked down to the shelf in the bookcase where there was an empty spot, exactly the right size for the annual. I slipped off the couch and knelt down on the floor and picked up the heavy book to replace it on the shelf. My hand hovered in front of the shelf. The light glinted off of the gold lettering on the binding, catching my eye. I sat down at the desk, dropped the yearbook into my lap, and stared down at the cover. It took a few minutes to find the courage to open the cover and flip through the pages.

The pages fell open to an unnatural crease in the binding. It took a couple seconds of scanning to realize why there was a crease on that particular page. The open page was the first of the sophomore class. There, in the third row, were the pictures of Rebecca and me. On the next page was a candid shot of us taken during lunch on a bench outside of the science building.

My eyes closed, vaguely remembering when the picture was taken. It had been two months after we began dating. Every last detail began to flood into my mind. Never in my life could I have imagined that a science class would change my life so much.

* * *

It was incomprehensible as to the extent that I hated biology. I sat at the large wooden table off to the side of the lab and ran my fingers over the smooth, black Formica surface. Dreaded images of what I assumed would be a long, boring year raced through my head. The musty ammonia scent of the room overpowered my nostrils, leading me to question why I had to be here. I was an artist, my calling in life, so I failed to see what purpose learning how plants converted light using photosynthesis or dissecting a frog would possibly be useful. It was my expert opinion that the class would be a huge waste of my time. There was just one minor problem with that logic—I was merely fifteen years old. What was I an expert at?

The door squeaked open behind me. I turned around expecting to see the teacher, Mr. Jennings, walk into the room. He was the kind of teacher that you had already heard stories about before you ever set foot in his classroom. Somewhat of an institution, Mr. Jennings had been the biology teacher for nearly thirty-five years. I was certain that nothing good would come out of this class, not after the stories I had heard.

Much to my surprise, it wasn't Mr. Jennings standing in the doorway. And in that single moment of time, I realized that I was not an expert at predicting where my time would be a waste. Standing in the doorway was the most beautiful girl that had ever graced my eyes. The light from the hallway fluorescents backlit her and gave her an almost angelic glow.

My eyes focused in on her as she stepped into the classroom. Her long brown hair—parted neatly in the middle with both sides tucked loosely behind her ears—hung down to nearly the middle of her back. She wore a sleeveless baby blue dress with white trim. Though her book bag was draped over her shoulders, she held a notebook close to her chest with her arms wrapped tightly, almost protectively, around it. She scanned the room for a seat and then walked toward my table. The closer she got, the harder it became for me to breathe. I held my breath and waited. She was, by far, the most attractive girl in the sophomore class and it seemed that she was coming to sit with me.

Attempting to be subtle, but only succeeding in being blatantly obvious, I slid my books closer to me to make it evident that the seat next to me was open. She walked up to my desk but, much to my surprise and dismay, continued past without so much as a pause. I could have sworn that I noticed a twinkle in her eye as she sat down at the adjacent table. There goes my shot, I thought to myself. She slipped her book bag off of her back and dropped it on the table, placing the notebook on top of the bag. I gave her the once over out of the corner of my eye. Seated, her dress showed off more of her lightly tanned legs. They were so enticing that I couldn't help but stare. Her skin looked so soft, so smooth, almost like a layer of silk was stretched over her bones. Somehow all of the muted light in the room seemed drawn to her skin, glowing as if it were a beacon in the darkness.

Lost in a daze, the classroom door opened again and yanked me out of my fantasy. I turned toward the door and there he was—Mr. Jennings. The stories I had heard were true so far. He was a very intimidating man and, just by looking at him, I could tell he was a stickler for the rules. His head was unusually small as if it stopped growing before the rest of his body, which looked like it had grown too much. Carrying close to three hundred pounds, he slid through the doorway and walked toward the front of the class. It wasn't until he set the briefcase on his desk that he showed even the slightest hint of emotion—a partial, almost obscure, smile.

As soon as the bell finished ringing, Mr. Jennings stepped around in front of his desk and removed a small manila folder from his briefcase. "Let's get started," he stated without emotion. "I have made a seating chart. So if you will pick up your things and stand, we can get this out of the way and start class."

Following along with the other students, I grabbed my book bag and notebook and stood up. We fell into lines with everyone else against the two side walls. Mr. Jennings began calling out names in alphabetical order. I knew I would be among the first called, since my last name started with a 'B'. Why couldn't my last name be further down in the alphabet? It always destined me to be stuck in the front row of every single class.

"Banks, Martin," Mr. Jennings called out.

"Yes, sir?" I stepped forward and raised my hand.

"Right here," he responded, pointing to the second table in the front row.

I walked toward the table, silently cursing my last name with each step. To get to my seat, I either had to walk behind Mr. Jennings' desk or squeeze past him in front of the desk. Obviously, I chose the former. I dropped my book bag on the floor and wondered who I would be stuck with as my lab partner for the entire year. I snuck a glance at the rest of the students standing along the wall. Just as I feared, halfway down the line was Allen Greenburg, the class nerd. At that moment I knew that I would be paired with him, alphabetical order or not, the same as in last year's physical science class. I sat watching Mr. Jennings as he looked down the roll sheet. He seemed to take his time calling out the next name. I held my breath, praying not to hear the word 'Greenburg.'

"Billings, Rebecca," Mr. Jennings called out.

My jaw dropped in shock. I was finally paired up with a girl instead of the class nerd. Not recognizing the name, I looked around the class to see who was heading toward my table. My heart just about stopped beating when I saw who she was.

Walking toward my table, radiating beauty and gracefulness with every step, positively glowing in her baby blue dress, was the girl whose name I now knew—Rebecca Billings.

I stared in awe at Rebecca during her entire walk to the table. Her soft brown hair bounced with each step she took. She had a beaming smile on her face. Her arms clutched her notebook to her chest, once again holding it tightly. My eyes drifted down to her legs, so graceful as she walked. The way she looked, especially if she kept wearing clothes such as she had on now, was going to make for an extremely distracting year.

Mr. Jennings continued calling out names from the seating chart as Rebecca sat down next to me. She placed her notebook on the table and then set her book bag on the floor. She looked over at me and grinned, catching me staring.

"Hi, I'm Rebecca," she said with an unnatural, but comforting, enthusiasm.

I froze for a second, not realizing that I needed to say something back. "Oh, I'm, um, I'm…Martin," I stammered. "Yeah, that's me."

"Well, that's good to hear," she said then directed her attention to her notebook as she flipped through the pages.

Yeah, that's me? What kind of idiotic response was that? I usually didn't have problems talking to anyone, even people I didn't know. But somehow this was different. I was at a complete loss for words. I scanned my brain, trying to come up with a topic that might be of interest to her. But I could think of nothing. Eventually, I just blurted out the first thing that came to mind.

"This should be an interesting year, don't you think?"

Rebecca closed her notebook and looked over at me. A slight twinkle lit her soft blue eyes. "Why do you say that?"

"Just some of the stories that I've heard about Mr. Jennings," I whispered, not wanting to be heard by anyone else. It would have been terrible to end up on the teacher's blacklist on the first day of class.

"Oh, well, I haven't heard any stories," she whispered back. "I just moved here from Atlanta with my family two weeks ago."

I should have seen that coming, I thought to myself. Of course she had to be the new girl. I had never seen her around before. I tried to think of something to salvage the conversation.

"Oh, how do you like Wilmington so far?"

"It's not bad," she answered. "Pretty different from Atl—"

"I'd like to welcome you all to biology. My name is Mr.

Jennings." Apparently, Mr. Jennings had finished calling names for the seating chart. I hadn't noticed that he had made his way back to the front and was now standing beside his desk. "I hope that this will be an informative and enlightening year for all of you." He opened his textbook to the first page.

I wish I could say that after class I walked with Rebecca and talked about all sorts of things, but I can't. The truth is that when the bell rang to dismiss class, I had a complete mental block. I couldn't think of one single thing to say to her so I resolved not to even approach her so as not to make more of a complete fool of myself than I already had. For the next week our conversations were limited to biology-related topics while sitting at our table. I would see her walking through the halls, but the best I could manage was a simple "Hi" when she passed by.

That continued into the middle of the following week, and I came to the unfortunate conclusion that was how it was going to be for the rest of the year. But then everything changed. I got to class early and was sitting at the table reading the textbook out of sheer boredom. Rebecca walked into the room and sat down at the table without any greeting or acknowledgement. One look at her face told me that something was wrong. Her usual beaming smile was disturbingly absent. I waited a second, trying to assess the situation before I spoke.

"Hi," I said.

"Hi," came her response. I waited for a moment, but she just sat there in silence.

"Is everything okay?" I asked.

"It's fine," Rebecca said, not even turning to look at me. "It's just that—" She cut herself off mid-sentence and her head dropped a little as she pressed her lips into a tight line.

I leaned in closer to her, wanting to put a consoling hand on her shoulder, but instead I just offered the first words that came to mind. "Yeah, I don't buy that. What's wrong?"

She leaned back in her chair and took a deep breath. "It's just that I was talking to my sister before school today. She was all excited about this boy she has a crush on. And I just saw him walking with some girl, holding hands." She turned toward me, looking up at me with her big, baby blue eyes, their usual twinkle gone. "So now I have to tell my sister. She's going to be devastated."

I tried to think of an adequate response, but I was at a loss. "Maybe it's not what it looked like," was all I could say.

"I don't know what else it could be," Rebecca replied.

"I take it that you and your sister are really close?"

"Very close, Kelly's my best friend."

I'm not sure if it was what she said or how she acted, but I knew in that moment that this girl was special. The fact that she could care so much about someone else was very moving. I wanted to say something that would make her feel better, to bring back that smile that I had grown accustomed to seeing on a daily basis, but nothing came to mind.

"Maybe you could talk to him, or something."

"Do you have any brothers or sisters?" she asked.

"No. I'm an only child."

"That explains it." She paused for a second, as if contemplating whether to continue with her thought. "If I went up and asked him about it, then he would know that Kelly liked him. That would embarrass her."

I couldn't help but stare at her while she talked, lost in her mesmerizing eyes. It wasn't until after she was silent for a few seconds that I noticed she had stopped talking and was looking at me, catching me staring…again. I glanced down at my textbook before looking back over at her.

"Well, if there's anything I can do to help, just let me know," I said.

"Thank you." She smiled at me. "That's really sweet of you."

I nodded and just sat there, torn between two extremes. I was pleased that because of me she had smiled. But I hated that she had called me sweet. No guy wanted to be called sweet or to be thought of as "a great guy" or "a good friend" by the girl he was interested in. It became my goal to make her see that even sweet guys still made good dates.

*　*　*

My eyes drifted back to the picture once again. A single tear escaped my eye and rolled down my cheek. I wiped it away with the back of my hand then closed the yearbook and placed it back on the shelf.

Pushing myself up from the chair, I made my way into the kitchen and poured a cup of coffee from the pot that Kelly had brewed earlier. The newspaper lay open on the kitchen table. I sat down and glanced over the headlines as I sipped the lukewarm coffee and waited for Kelly to return from her run.

Chapter Thirteen

The next two days passed by with an antagonizing slowness. On the outside it might have looked like I was doing nothing but staring into space, but inside my mind raced with a ferocious intensity. The vacant look in my eyes served to mask what was happening beneath. I felt furious over losing Rebecca, rage for having her taken so abruptly from me, fear over being alone, and resentment for everyone who still had the person that they loved or held dear.

Since Kelly could pick up on my various moods, she knew when to hold back and when it was safe to talk to me. I was sitting on the couch during one of my calmer moments when she approached and eased down next to me.

"We need to talk," she said.

In that instant, I knew exactly what she wanted to talk about. It was only a matter of time before the topic came up. With my gaze locked on the empty screen of the television in front of me, I beat her to the punch. "So when are you leaving?" My head turned to look at her only after I spoke.

"How did you know?"

"I knew that you weren't going to stay here forever. The time was coming when you would go back home. It was inevitable."

"I guess so. I just didn't want to leave without knowing that you would be okay on your own. I mean, I can stay another couple of days, or whatever. It's really not a problem. There's no rush for me to go home. I can stay as long as you need me to."

My lips pressed together as the corners of my mouth curved upward in a halfhearted smile. "No, you should go. Really. It's fine. You've already done so much already. And I've already kept you from your own family far too long." Then as an afterthought, "I know, I know. You don't have to say it. We've been over it already. 'But Martin, you are a part of my family. And you always will be.'"

Kelly shook her head as she rolled her eyes, flashing feigned annoyance. She reached over and caressed my forearm. "Well, I'm glad I hammered that point into your thick skull. But seriously, I mean it. After I'm gone, if you ever need anything, anything at all, or you just want to talk, call me anytime, day or night."

"I appreciate that, really. And believe me, if I ever need anything, you'll be the first person that I call. I know I've said it plenty of times already, but there's no way I can fully thank you for everything you've done around here the past month."

"Hey, don't worry about it. I'm sure you would have done the same for me if I had needed help. Besides, that's what family is for, right?"

"I suppose so. I just feel bad because you are the only family I have left now. I mean, both of my parents are gone, and now Rebecca, so who else do I have to turn to?"

"You'll always have both Mark and me. You can count on us for anything."

I smiled at Kelly then let my head fall back on the couch. Kelly settled back beside me, her hand still resting on my arm. I reached over and patted the back of her hand.

"Oh, you never did answer," I continued. "When were you going to leave?"

"I didn't? Oh, yeah, I guess not. Um, I was thinking about tomorrow afternoon."

We sat there in silence for a moment before Kelly got up and walked into the kitchen to get started on dinner. I glanced down at my watch after she left. It was nearly five. Another wasted day. I heard Kelly rummaging around the pantry, pushing items aside as if she were searching for something specific.

"Anything in particular that you want to eat?" she asked.

I felt the onset of one of my moods. The last thing I wanted to do was to take anything out on her. I pushed up from the couch and headed for the front door, grabbing my jacket from the closet.

"I'm not really hungry," I called back over my shoulder. "I think I'll go for a walk. I'll be back in a bit."

The door squeaked as I pulled it shut. I stopped on the porch and stared out over the water. The cool air from the incoming cold front blew against my face. I closed my eyes and remained motionless on the porch as the air wrapped its frigid hands around me. Sparked with a sudden rejuvenation, I headed down the steps and blew into my cupped hands to ward off the chill.

The ocean looked like a tumultuous layer of liquid iron with foaming metal waves crashing at my feet. I walked south down the shore toward a small rock jetty. Each step on the jetty was precarious. One slip and I could fall headlong into the water. I jumped across a gap to the last boulder and sat on one of the larger rocks with my feet dangling over the side just above a small alcove of calm water. The waves crashed into the jetty and sent a misty spray of saltwater against my face. I remained sitting, facing out toward the water, eyes sometimes open, sometimes closed. Behind me, the sun carved its downward path toward the horizon. All around me, the shadows grew longer in the fleeting light.

It seemed to me that everyone should have a place where they can go to retreat within their own thoughts, a place to be alone and undisturbed. A few lucky people had more than one of these places. I counted myself among the fortunate who had multiple private spots. When I was at home, I could always find solitude within the comforts of my studio. But over the past month that had changed. I no longer found solace in my painting nor in the room.

In the weeks since closing the studio, I had been unable to find any comfort at home, especially now being alone in the house. Granted Kelly was still here, but it wasn't the same. I knew she was leaving in a day and, after that, I would truly be alone. I guess it was ironic. I would be alone in the house, which was what people looked for in solitude, but I would not be at peace in it. So the ongoing quest for solitude had led me to my jetty. It was right on the water, yet not the beach. Sitting out here made me feel like I was detached from the world, somewhere in my own place, all to myself. Though it was in plain sight, it was not a place that many people visited. Most people walked right past it without so much as a second glance. That alone made it the perfect place for me when I didn't want to be bothered.

Time became irrelevant. I could stay for five minutes or five hours. Except for my own thoughts, the rest of the world seemed to fade away. Even the ocean dissolved into a surreal emptiness and became nothing but a shimmering, ambiguous mass of ever-changing colors and shapes. All around me a shadow loomed, growing larger and dominating the view. Something reached out toward me but remained just out of focus. My gaze followed the vague black object for a moment. I snapped out of my illusion to find that Kelly stood behind me with her arm hovering just over my shoulder. She pulled her hand back when I turned my head toward her and she sat down on the slab of rock next to me.

We sat in silence for a moment, gazing out over the water before she looked over at me. "You've been out here for a while. I just wanted to check and make sure you were okay. I was starting to worry."

The time spent just sitting here thinking had calmed my earlier mood. I was placated, no doubt the result of the soothing water around me. "I'm okay," I answered, my eyes never leaving the ocean, "...now."

Kelly sat looking at me, but I said nothing else and just continued to gaze out toward the horizon. She pushed herself to her feet and looked down at me before turning to head back up the jetty.

"Wait a second," I called out, rising to my feet as well. "I'm sorry for making you worry. I really didn't mean to do that."

"I know and I understand. Really I do. This is a rough time you're going through right now. Just know that I'm here for you. Whatever you need, all you have to do is ask."

I maneuvered over the path of the jagged rocks to catch up

with Kelly. We trekked across the jetty toward the beach.

"I don't know how you do it," I said as I took Kelly's hand to help her hop from one stone to the next.

She paused on the edge of the boulder and raised an eyebrow. "What are you talking about?"

"Just how you seem to be so strong about everything. You and Rebecca were so much alike in that. She was more concerned with me the last month than with herself. And now the way you are, being so strong and helping me out with everything. It's like you are in complete control of your own emotions."

Kelly gripped my hand tighter and squeezed her eyes shut as she shook her head. "I'm not as strong as you think I am. It just appears that way." Her eyes opened and she stared straight into my eyes with an inviting, yet fire-like, intensity. "I'm going to let you in on a little secret. What you see is a façade. I have cried and mourned for my sister as much as the next person. The only difference is that I did it alone. All those early morning runs weren't just because I like to keep in shape. Every time I disappeared back into my room to read, or whatever, I didn't always start reading immediately."

My eyebrow curved upward as I repeated her words to myself. "Why?" was the only thing I could manage to say.

"I thought it was obvious. Because of you," Kelly paused long enough to hop across the small gorge between the rocks. She released my hand and turned to face me from across the chasm. "I knew you were taking it really hard and that you needed something, or someone, strong to lean on. I was that person. I had to be strong so that you could deal with it."

"But you did that at the expense of your own grieving."

"I'll be able to grieve, trust me. When I leave to go home,

I'll have Mark and the kids to help me deal with things, but you, you'll be alone. It's what you needed from me before I left so that..." She stopped mid-thought after seeing the expression on my face. "I'm sorry. I shouldn't have said it that way, talking about having my family to help me."

I forced a smile and looked out over the water. "No, you're right. I should know by now that you're always right. It was what I needed and I really appreciate everything you've done."

"Are you okay?"

"I'm fine, really." I jumped across the gap to join her on the rock. We continued to make our way along the jetty and finally emerged back on the sandy beach. The short walk up the beach to the house passed by in silence.

*   *   *

After eating dinner and cleaning up the kitchen, Kelly and I retreated into the living room and sat down on the couch. The only light in the room came from a single lamp on the end table beside the couch and two small candles on the coffee table. The dim light cast long shadows across the room. We just sat there for a few minutes staring at the ever-changing, flickering shadows.

"There's something I wanted to ask you, but I don't know if now is the right time to ask, or if I should even ask at all," Kelly blurted out.

"No, it's ok. Go ahead and ask."

Kelly stared at me for a moment then looked down at her hands folded in her lap. She picked at one of her nails, not speaking until she finished and gave her hand a thorough inspection. Her eyes reflected a shimmering reflection when she looked over at me. "Do you ever regret not having kids?"

My head fell back hard against the couch as the air rushed

out of my lungs. "Wow, you weren't kidding when you said you were unsure of asking me, were you?"

"We don't have to talk about it if it makes you uncomfortable."

"It's fine, really. It caught me off-guard, that's all."

"That's understandable. It was just something that had been on my mind lately."

"Well, yeah, sometimes I regret that we didn't have children. But I guess that some people are meant to have a family while it's not in the cards for others. Don't get me wrong. It's not like we didn't try or didn't want to have kids. It just never happened. I guess it was bad timing or something. We never really talked in-depth about why we never had kids. We did talk about the possibilities of having them early on, right after we got married. Why do you ask?"

Kelly turned her head away and stared at the wall. Her expression changed. Her thoughts became even more unreadable. I slid over on the couch closer to her and slipped my arm around her shoulders.

"Hey, what's wrong? What's going on?"

Kelly shuddered under my arm. The traces of a single vein in her neck rose from the surface of the skin, throbbing from the pulsing blood beneath. Her jaw locked in place with her teeth clenched together. I took note of the sudden changes and braced myself for whatever Kelly was about to say.

"Bec and I talked a lot the last couple of weeks about so many things. One of the topics we kept going back to was children. Asking me what it was like having kids and having a family like I do."

I felt my own jaw tightening and the veins in my neck throbbing. My hand balled up into a fist in my lap.

Kelly took a deep breath before continuing. "She would always ask a couple of questions, and then change the subject to something else. It wasn't until the last time we talked about it that she finally told me why she kept bringing it up. She said that one of the things she regretted was not having kids with you. I think she believed that if you guys would have had kids of your own, then none of this would have happened. But more than that, she knew that if you had kids, she wouldn't have been so scared of leaving you alone."

I fought off the spontaneous glaze of tears that was building up. "Why would she think that?"

"It's common knowledge that conceiving and giving birth drastically reduces the likelihood for a woman to be diagnosed with ovarian cancer. I guess she felt that if she had gotten pregnant and had a baby that none of this would have happened."

A horrifying thought ran through my mind. Bec blamed herself for this. She thought it was all her fault. My fingernails dug into the soft flesh of my balled-up palm.

Kelly looked over at me through red-rimmed eyes. Tears streamed down her cheeks in waves. As if on cue, a tear escaped my eye and carved a path down my own cheek, dripping off of my clenched jaw and landing with a minute splash on my arm.

I had tried to be strong through the whole ordeal from the second we found out that Rebecca had cancer. It seemed that was what I needed to do at the time, what Rebecca needed from me. I hadn't even cried at the funeral. It had taken everything I had to hold things together. I had built a wall around myself that kept my emotions bottled up inside. The wall was my strength. But over time, even the strongest wall can be weakened and brought down by the elements. In one fell swoop, my entire wall came crashing down by the flood of on-coming tears that had built up over the past month.

Kelly leaned into me and buried her face in my chest. We both wrapped our arms around each other and held on with all we had. It had been almost a week since the funeral, but this was the first time I had allowed myself to grieve. Before the funeral, I had tried to remain strong for Rebecca. After the funeral, it had been for Kelly and out of anger. The reasons were the same for her, as well. But those reasons suddenly seemed irrelevant as we sat crying. Absolutely nothing else mattered.

*   *   *

The morning welcomed me with the soft crash of waves on the packed sand. Several birds chirped right outside my window. Their soothing sounds had pulled me out of a dreamless sleep. Everything after Kelly and I began crying on the couch last night was a complete blur. I wasn't sure when, or how, I got to bed, but I did know that I got a decent night's sleep for the first time in weeks.

As I lay in bed it occurred to me that the act of grieving was a very interesting process. No two people grieved in the same way. Some people needed only a matter of minutes to finish while it took others months, or even years, to complete the process. Likewise, it was a different experience for each person. Some people grieved and moved on easily while others grieved but never really moved on. It was hard, if not impossible, to predict which would happen. Now that I had allowed the grieving process to begin, I had absolutely no idea how things would continue to play out in my life. Everything was uncertain and up in the air. The only thing that I was sure of was that Kelly was leaving in a couple of hours.

I pushed myself to my feet and stumbled toward the bathroom. A few minutes later I made my way out through the living room and into the kitchen. Kelly was already up and had just started brewing a pot of coffee. She sat at the kitchen table skimming through the paper.

"Morning," I greeted her as I stopped in front of the coffee pot, inhaling to allow the aroma of the brewing coffee to finish waking me up. "Are you all packed?"

She glanced toward the living room. There, next to the couch, were two small suitcases. I had been oblivious to them as I entered the kitchen moments earlier.

"Almost," she answered. "I only have a few more things to get together, mainly the toiletries and stuff."

"When were you thinking of heading out?"

"I was shooting for after breakfast. That way I can be home and unpacked before the kids get home from school."

I nodded at her and then grabbed two coffee cups from the rack next to the pot. Steam floated up toward my face as I poured a cup from the freshly brewed pot. I handed the cup to Kelly then poured another cup for myself and joined her at the table. We sipped our coffee and skimmed through the paper. Kelly finished the last section and set it down in front of me then jumped up and began rummaging through the fridge.

"It's okay," I said, setting the paper down on the table. "You don't have to fix anything. I'm not really that hungry."

"It's not a problem. Besides, I wouldn't want to leave without making sure you had a decent meal to start off the day."

"Well, if you insist."

I leaned back in the chair and grabbed the last section of the paper, reading as Kelly fixed breakfast. The meal passed with not a single word spoken. After eating, I cleaned the dishes as

Kelly headed back into her room to finish gathering her things.

She emerged carrying a small overnight bag. I stood up and grabbed her two suitcases from behind the couch and carried them to the door.

We walked outside to her car. I put the suitcases in the trunk while Kelly dropped the overnight bag in the back seat.

"You sure you have everything?"

She looked around at her bags. "Yeah, I've got everything."

I stepped around the back of the car and extended my arms. Kelly fell against me and wrapped her arms around my waist.

"Call me when you get home, okay?"

"I will." She paused, her brown eyes piercing deep into me. "Are you going to be okay?"

"I'll be fine. Don't you worry about me."

"I can't help it. You're family, remember?"

I shook my head as the smallest smile squeezed through my pressed lips. "Yeah, yeah, now get out of here and go home."

"You call me if you need anything. Anything at all."

We hugged once more before she opened the door and slid behind the wheel. She cranked the ignition and rolled down the front window.

"Be safe," I leaned down and said.

Kelly smiled at me as she put the car in gear and backed out of the driveway, waving as she pulled out on the street. I returned her wave and remained standing in the driveway as she sped down the road. Long after her car disappeared from view, I remained in the driveway, looking out over the water. A single thought passed through my mind as I turned to head inside.

Now, I was truly all alone.

Chapter Fourteen

In all my years, I had never seen someone enjoy a hot meal when they were sad or depressed. Following suit, I was eating cold pizza straight from the box, leftover from the night before. The dim light of the muted television pierced through the darkness and sent dancing shadows across the barren walls. I took a bite of the cold pizza with one hand as I flipped through the channels on the remote with the other in a welcomed distraction from the mundane existence that plagued me.

Since Kelly left four days ago—well even before that, since the funeral, I hadn't wanted to do anything. If it involved going outside it was too much of a chore and was put off until later, even though I knew it would never be taken care of later.

A quick glance toward the wall clock told me that it was almost seven. Normally, that wouldn't make a difference, since the only television I watched at night was the local news. I would paint until dinner, and then afterward I would do something with Rebecca or read a book. But that was all over now. It seemed that all I had been doing lately was sitting in front of the TV, stuck in a trance and blindly watching whatever it played. I stopped flipping channels on an old black and white movie that caught my eye. Just before I pressed the button to un-mute the sound, I heard faint footsteps climbing up the front steps. I disregarded them and pressed the button to allow the sound of the movie to fill the room.

The chiming of the doorbell rang throughout the house. I sat, unmoving, on the couch, hoping that whoever the visitor was would just go away. Then the knocking began. The frustration grew inside me. I put the half-eaten piece of pizza back in the box and tossed the remote on the couch as I stood up and walked toward the door. As I reached the foyer, there was another knock at the door.

"Take it easy. I'm coming," I called out. My hand seized the doorknob and I yanked the door open. There, half-hidden in the shadows of the porch, stood Paul Taylor, Leslie's father. He stepped forward holding out his hand to me with a strained smile on his face. I stared at the figure in front of me, not believing he was there. Even as I reached out to take his hand, I still thought it was a dream. It was not until my hand firmly grasped Paul's that I believed he was not another apparition.

"Hey, Martin," Paul greeted me with his trademark baritone voice.

"Paul?" My expression of surprise turned into one of confusion. "What are you doing here?"

"I was in the area on business for a couple of days and wanted to stop by and see how you were doing. Besides, I didn't know I needed a reason to visit."

"You never need a reason to come by. It just caught me off-guard for a second. I didn't expect it."

"Don't worry about it," Paul said, smiling. "So…how are

you doing?"

I glanced around the foyer as I answered. "I'm existing, that's about the extent of it."

Paul leaned forward and poked his head through the doorway, eyeing the foyer. Not much had changed in regards to the appearance of the house in the year or so since Paul had last visited. Never moving from his spot on the porch, he kept looking around. It took me a second to realize what he was hinting at.

"Oh, you want to come in?"

With a sheepish grin, Paul stepped through the door. "I thought you'd never ask."

I moved aside as Paul passed through the foyer toward the living room. I followed him in and fell back down on the couch. Paul sat in the chair across from me.

"So what brings you to town again?"

"Well, I was in Wilmington last week, checking in on the parents and doing a little negotiation. Then I had to come down here to check on a new contract."

"Yeah, Leslie was telling me about that. Something about a new project in Beaufort?"

"Yeah, actually it's at Parris Island. I won the bid for building the new Marine barracks."

"That's great," I exclaimed. "That's only a few minutes away from the shop." After finishing the sentence, my expression dropped. Paul seemed to notice the change in my demeanor.

"I'm sorry I wasn't here for you. I was in Buffalo at a trade convention and a sudden front pushed in over the Lakes dumping four feet of snow. Some freak lake-effect storm. All flights were grounded for almost three days. O'Hare was even out of commission for a day."

"It's okay. I didn't want to be there myself."

Paul shifted in the chair. "How are you holding up?"

"Not too well."

"Well, you look terrible."

I looked over at him, not sure if I heard him right. It didn't seem possible that he just said what I thought he said. But it all became clear when I saw the look on his face. Paul gave me his best attempt at a grin after trying to lighten the mood.

"Hey, thanks a lot," I responded as I stood up.

"Have you been out since then?"

"No, not unless the front porch and beach count." I stepped toward the kitchen and called back over my shoulder. "Do you want something to drink?"

"Please," he answered. "What do you have?"

As soon as I opened the refrigerator, I regretted making the offer. The fridge was still decently stocked with food, but beverages were virtually non-existent. Most of the containers were nearing empty, but I finally spied a couple cans of soda hidden behind all the food and headed back to the living room.

"Um, I've got Coke and Coke."

"I'll take a Coke then," Paul answered.

I handed one of the cans to Paul then took my seat on the couch. We popped open our cans and the rush of escaping air and carbonation echoed through the room. We took several sips before resuming the conversation. An hour later, we were still talking. Both cans of Coke had long since been finished. I excused myself and scrounged around the pantry in the kitchen, scoring a few more drinks. After pouring the drinks into cups and adding some ice, I returned to the living room. Paul stood next to the window, looking out at the dark sky.

"It's beautiful, isn't it?" I said, handing a glass to Paul.

"Absolutely amazing," he responded. "It sort of reminds me of that time we all drove down to Caswell Beach after we graduated."

"Yeah, I took Bec back down to that lighthouse the day after I proposed to her."

Paul backed away from the window and turned toward me. The look on his face was apology enough, but he still offered up a verbal one as well. "I'm sorry. I didn't mean to..."

"Don't worry about it."

"You sure?"

"Yeah, there's almost nothing that we can talk about that doesn't remind me of her. Everywhere I go, everything I do, I see her."

Paul sat back down on the couch. "That's got to be really hard."

I remained next to the window, sliding over to take Paul's vacated spot. The moon peeked over the horizon and cast a brilliant reflection over the rippling waves.

"It is," I answered. "And the worst part is waking up every morning, knowing she's not there. I'm not complete without her. I can't live without her."

The couch groaned as Paul leaned forward. "What are you saying?"

I turned away from the window to face Paul. "I'm saying that...I don't really know what I'm saying," I admitted. "Something that was a part of me for over thirty years is gone. How am I supposed to react to something like that?"

A slight shake of his head was the only response that Paul offered to me. He dropped his head and stared at the floor. I turned back toward the window and stared out over the ocean. My gaze shifted from the water to the wall where an old black and white photograph of the Oak Island Lighthouse was prominently displayed.

"You should have never gotten rid of that '67 Mustang convertible."

"Don't I know it," Paul agreed. "There are times when I kick myself for selling it after college. The one I bought last year just isn't the same."

"Did I ever tell you she spotted a satellite passing overhead that night?"

"You didn't."

The corners of my lips curved upward. "She thought it was a plane, but I told her what it was. Then she tried to argue that it was still a plane and I was wrong just because I'd never flown on one yet."

Paul laughed. "That definitely sounds like her."

"That whole time you and Christine were walking up the beach, me and Bec were staring up at the stars. I told her all about the mythology behind the constellations. Her favorite was the one about Andromeda." My gaze drifted from the photograph to the clear sky outside the window. "I must have told her the same story at least twenty times, but she always acted like it was the first time she had heard it."

"What was it?"

"The story goes that there was this beautiful Ethiopian princess, born to King Cepheus and Queen Cassiopeia. The Queen was a very boastful and vain woman. She went around bragging that her daughter, Andromeda, was more beautiful than even the sea nymphs. Now this claim insulted the Nereids, who took their case to Poseidon. He sent a great sea monster to destroy the kingdom to avenge his nymphs. Desperate to save his kingdom, Cepheus went to see the Oracle,

Ammon, who advised the King to sacrifice Andromeda to the monster in order to appease Poseidon and the nymphs. Reluctantly, Cepheus went about with the preparations by chaining his daughter to a cliff overlooking the water. It so happened that Perseus, the nephew of the King of Argos was on his journey back from killing Medusa. The second Perseus saw Andromeda he immediately fell in love with her. He found out the reason she was there and sought to prevent her from being sacrificed. Seeking an audience with the King, Perseus told Cepheus and Cassiopeia that he would kill the monster if they would allow him to marry Andromeda. They quickly agreed in order to save their daughter. So Perseus made his way back to the cliff as the sea monster approached. He held up the head of Medusa, turning the monster into stone, and thus saving Andromeda. She was released from her chains and soon thereafter married Perseus. After the wedding, Andromeda left the country with her new husband, who became King of another land. As a reward for keeping her parents' promise, the goddess Athena placed an image of Andromeda among the stars for all to see and marvel in her majestic beauty."

The story ended and silence hung over the two of us for several seconds.

"I can see why she loved the story."

"She said that it was a beautiful story and that she wished she could have an everlasting monument like that made for her." The words caught up in my throat. "I told her that I wasn't sure about putting her in the heavens, but I might be able to do something about creating a monument for her. That was the first time she asked me to paint her."

"Are you still painting now?"

"I haven't been able to pick up a brush since she died. It's just too hard for me."

Paul rose from the couch and stood next to me by the window. We both stood there looking through the darkness over the calm ocean. "So then what are you doing?"

I shook my head without glancing away from the water.

"You really need to get out and do something," Paul said. "It's not good for you to be shut off from the world like this."

"I'm not shut off. This is the first time I've actually been alone. Kelly was here until four days ago. Besides, I see the pizza delivery guy every other day."

"You know what I mean," Paul replied, failing to hide a smile.

"Nothing matters anymore."

"Look, we have a couple of contracts that are almost complete in Charleston. But we still need a few more painters. I know it's not what you've been doing, but I could pull some strings for you. I am tight with the boss after all."

"Thanks for the offer, but I can't paint, or even pick up a brush right now. It doesn't matter what kind of painting it is."

"I understand. I'm sure I could find you something that doesn't involve painting," Paul offered. "I just hate for you to be sitting here doing nothing all day."

I nodded my head in forced acknowledgement. It wasn't a bad thing to have Paul see about getting me a stint with one of the contracts his company had. Maybe he was right about me needing to get out of the house.

"Well, I should probably get going," Paul said. We both slowly walked toward the front door, pausing in the foyer.

I extended my hand to him. "Thanks for stopping by."

Paul grasped my hand. "Anytime, my friend."

"I'll talk to you later. Have a safe trip."

"I'll give you a call when I find something out about the jobs."

I nodded again as Paul stepped through the door. I flipped on the porch light as he made his way down the steps toward his car. After he backed down the driveway and pulled out onto the street, I flipped off the light and disappeared back into the prison of my house.

* * *

Paul called me two days later with the details of the job in Charleston. During that call he made another valid point about getting out. What was I supposed to do, just sit around the house and never leave again? I spent the next few weeks mulling over his offer before finally deciding to give his office a call. After reaching Paul's secretary at his office in Columbia, she told me that he was in a meeting and would be back in the office in a minute. I decided it was just as easy to wait the few minutes on hold as it would be for Paul to call me when he got back to the office.

The soft lull of Beethoven's 9th Symphony played in the background. I closed my eyes and let the music flow through me. My head swayed back and forth to the high-pitched, rapid violin beats. With a sudden click, the music was silenced.

"Martin!" rang Paul's voice through the line. "I'm really glad you called."

"How's it going?"

"No complaints here. Why didn't you just call my cell? It's easier to get in touch with me that way."

"I figured that since it was a business call, I would just go through your office. Besides, you were in a meeting and I didn't want to interrupt."

"You've never been in a business meeting, have you?" Paul

snickered over the line, and, without waiting for my answer, he continued. "Any interruption during a business meeting is a welcome occurrence, believe me. If they weren't a requirement of being the boss, I'd never be caught in one again."

A laugh escaped under my breath before I was able to catch it. I paused hoping that it turned out to be inaudible.

"You think I'm joking, don't you? You just wait. I'll drag you into one of my board meetings if it's the last thing I do." His cackling laugh echoed through the receiver. "But that's not why you called, is it?"

"No, it's not," I answered, pausing to collect my thoughts. "I've thought about what you said over the past two weeks, and decided to take you up on your offer. If it's still open, that is."

I could literally hear the smile form on Paul's face before he had a chance to respond. "Of course it's still open. And I'm glad you decided to take it. Um, when did you want to start?"

"Whenever you need me to. I'm pretty open."

"How about Monday?" Paul suggested. "I'll call the project manager up in Charleston and take care of everything. When you show up Monday, all you'll have to do is sign a few papers then you can get straight to work. How's that?"

"That works for me."

"Good, I'll have him call you to let you know when and where. Oh, and I'll make sure you get added to the Parris Island crew doing the Marine barracks. I can always use good people."

The nervousness in the pit of my stomach began to settle down for the first time in a week. I really don't know why I had been so uneasy in the first place. Maybe it was because I was taking the first steps in moving on with my life.

"Hey Paul, thanks a lot. For everything."

"Anytime. I'm just glad I could help."

"Well, I really appreciate it. But I'll let you get back to work now. Don't want to tie up anymore of your time, boss man."

"I'm going to be making a trip down there next week to see how things are going. Plus, we ran into some complications at one of the other sites. While I'm there, maybe Leslie, you, and I can get together for dinner, or something."

"Sounds good to me. I'll see you then."

With a click, the line went dead. I dropped the receiver back in the cradle and leaned against the kitchen doorframe.

*   *   *

Monday morning rolled around and I made the hour drive to Charleston to start my first day of work. It felt strange to be leaving the house to go to work. I couldn't remember having a job outside the house since, well, ever in my life. My daily ritual had always been to get up, eat, and then go into my studio to start painting. The closest I had ever been to working outside the house was when I decided to throw the easel and canvas in the trunk of the car and drove around until I found something interesting to paint. The changing of the times hit me as I neared the end of the drive. Everything was different now, and it would never be the same again.

I pulled onto the side street off of East Bay Street in the historic district a couple of minutes before eight. The entire block was a flurry of construction activity. I found the site for the law offices where I would be working. A space was open next to a beat-up old truck with a tool rack setup in the bed that would make even Bob Vila jealous. I made my way toward a mobile trailer on the side of the street that served as the construction unit's headquarters. The project manager and the crew chief stepped out just as I reached the building and I introduced my-self. I filled out the proper forms then was ushered through the door for the tour around the site.

"Have you ever worked in construction before?" Chris, the crew chief, asked as we stepped through the empty doorway into the shell of a building.

"Not exactly, but I did do a complete remodel of my house down in Edisto. And I have helped families in my church do some work around their houses, building decks and whatnot."

"Well that should be good enough to get you off to a running start."

The interior walls consisted only of the two-by-four studs. A stack of drywall rested in the middle of the floor. A crew of three men was busy hanging the new panels of drywall. The men paused long enough for Chris to introduce them to me then they were back to work.

"This is the crew you'll be on," Chris told me. "Donald is in charge, so just do whatever he says and things will be good to go."

After a quick goodbye, Chris hurried out of the building and back to the trailer. One of the men worked with me so that we had two crews of two hanging the drywall panels. By the end of the day, we had the entire interior of the second floor of the building finished.

The burning sensation that coursed through my legs as I walked to my car reminded me of how easy my life had been when I painted. I never had to worry about aching muscles or stiff limbs. The biggest problem I faced was finding a new sub-ject to capture among the plentiful landscape. On occasion, my arm would get tired from holding the brush up to the canvas, but that would be remedied by switching hands and letting the other rest.

The drive home seemed much longer than it had earlier that morning. As I passed through Hollywood, I knew that I would be too tired to fix something when I got home, so I stopped at a small diner to grab dinner.

The sun had already descended behind the tree line by the time I pulled into the driveway. The last rays of the day streaked through the cloudless sky. I never did like a clear evening sky. It always seemed so devoid of life and color. With a plain blue sky, all you have is blue. But with a cloud-filled sky, when the sun sets, you have all the various shades of blue, orange, red, yellow and purple. It was the plethora of colors that made the most perfect of sunsets.

I paused halfway up the front steps to look out over the blackening water and then behind me over the treetops at the colorless sky. Night was rolling in. The setting made for a very dreary view. A few steps later, I was inside the house where the mood was not much different than it had been outside.

The next morning came much earlier than desired. I woke up and repeated the events of the previous day. At the job site, my crew was doing the same job but on a different floor. With two of the four floors that made up the one building still lacking interior walls, I knew that hanging the drywall would be my daily task until at least the end of the week.

It wasn't a bad job or a hard one for that matter. It was just very boring and monotonous work. It wasn't like I could be creative and develop some new, revolutionary method to hang drywall, nor would I even want to try. I looked at this as just a job, not a career. It was just something to do that provided me with a source of income since I no longer painted.

Not only were my days repetitive, but even my nights were

the same. I ended up stopping at the same diner for dinner on my way home from work. It wasn't until Thursday night that there was any change in my routine. After making a quick trip to Charleston to attend meetings regarding some issues at one of the other job sites, Paul stopped by the job site Thursday afternoon to check on the progress. And true to his promise, Paul, Leslie and I met for dinner that night.

A little before six-thirty, I stopped in front of Hyman's Seafood, a small local place in the historic district. The building looked more like a storefront than a restaurant. A huge plate-glass window opened into the dining area.

The second I walked in the door I was greeted by Jasmine, an overly joyful waitress with a beaming smile on her face. I told her that there would be two more people joining me. She led me beneath the pale, white rafters, along the red brick walls, and to a table in the corner, just past the black, wrought-iron spiral staircase. As I sat down, she took my drink order and scampered off toward the kitchen. I sat at the table, looking around the room. Dozens of white china plates hung on the walls.

Paul and Leslie arrived right as Jasmine returned with my drink. They saw me sitting in the corner and waved, then made their way across the room to join me. Jasmine took their drink orders and hurried back into the kitchen, returning a minute later with their drinks and three menus.

"I'll give you a chance to look at the menus and come back in a couple minutes," she said to us before leaving to check on another table.

"So how are things?" Paul asked me after the waitress left the table.

"Yeah, how's the new job? The boss isn't being too much

of a slave driver, I hope." Leslie shot a toothy smile at her dad and winked.

"No, it's not too bad. Much more physically demanding than my old job was."

Paul flashed a mischievous grin at me with a slight twinkle in his eye. "Well, what job isn't more physically demanding?"

"I can't argue with that. I'm still trying to adapt to the whole idea of leaving the house to go to work. You wouldn't believe how hard of a concept that is after nearly forty years of working from home."

Jasmine returned to the table and took our meal orders. I decided on the Charleston Crab Cakes while Paul ordered the Buffalo Shrimp. Leslie went with the Seafood Fettuccini Marinara. After taking our orders, Jasmine disappeared back into the kitchen. Paul's eyes drifted around the room.

"I'm thinking about opening up a small chain of restaurants like this up in Wilmington, tying into the historic areas," Paul stated. "What do you think?"

Leslie nodded her approval. "It sounds like a great idea to me. I love this place. I try to stop by every couple of weeks."

I gazed around the crowded room. Nearly every table was occupied, as was the case with every stool at the bar. "Seems like it would be a good investment to me."

"Speaking of investments and businesses, how's the store running?"

I looked first at Paul then over at Leslie. It was unclear as to whether he was asking me or her the question. But Leslie spoke up in response. "It's doing well. We're in the off-season, so it's not as busy as the summer. We have a steady base of local clients that provide enough business."

"That's good to hear. You have a nice little investment

there, Martin. Local shops in seasonal tourist areas that manage to stay open and successful year round are a rarity."

I had been dreading this moment. The decision had been weighing on my mind about what to do with the shop. I had a couple of options, neither of which seemed to be the right decision, but neither could be ruled out.

"Yeah, about that…I'm not really sure if I'm going to keep the shop."

Leslie's gaze fixed on me, her eyes mirroring the confusion obviously tearing at her mind after my shocking revelation. She glanced over at Paul, who stared at me with one eyebrow raised.

"Why wouldn't you keep it?" Paul asked.

"The store was never really mine. It was always Rebecca's thing. And I know that I'll never set foot in the building again." I could tell that neither Paul, nor Leslie, really understood what I was trying to say. "This has been something that I've been thinking about for the past couple of weeks." As the words came out of my mouth, it seemed like a convincing argument, but who exactly was I trying to convince…them or me?

"Have you completely thought this through?" Paul asked me, his voice unable to hide his concern.

"I'd like to think I have. Why?"

"It just seems to me that the shop is a good investment to have." Paul glanced over toward Leslie and smiled. "Not to mention, it would save my daughter her job."

The consequences of my decisions were in front of me. If I closed or sold the shop it wouldn't just affect me. It would affect Leslie and the handful of other employees.

"Well, what do you suggest?"

"As I said before, it's a good money-maker, especially since it has a year-round market. And that gives you a supplementary income. I mean, you don't want to be working for me the rest of your life, do you?"

Paul had a convincing argument and he was right that I didn't want to work in construction for the rest of my life. I hated the fact that I hadn't thought this out completely before mentioning it to them.

"I guess you have a point."

"Of course I have a point. Don't I always?"

"Yeah, yeah. So what exactly are you suggesting that I do?"

"First of all, don't sell or close down the shop. Keep it open as usual, but then that poses a new problem. How will you keep everything in order without having to go there yourself? The answer is your new manager sitting right here at the table. Am I right in assuming that going back to the shop will bring back memories for you?" I nodded. "So you keep working for me, or stay at home and do nothing. But have Leslie run the store. It allows her to keep her job and gives you a good investment and a decent source of supplemental income."

Paul flashed his wide smile at me from across the table. All I could do was shake my head.

"I don't know how you do it."

"Do what?"

"You have a knack for coming up with these arguments and proposals on the spot, or off the cuff, however you want to describe it. Rebecca was like that, too." My eyes clouded over.

Paul leaned forward over the table. "Let me tell you a little secret." I nodded for him to go on, hoping he could avert the disaster building in my mind. "I usually just start talking as my mind formulates the plan. Then I spend the rest of the conversation figuring out how to make my plan work. So, it's not like

I had this all planned out before I suggested it. I actually thought out most of the logic about five seconds before I said it."

"Well, still." I smiled. "I don't know how you do it."

Leslie looked across the table at me. I could see the worry in her eyes as she asked, "So do I still have a job?"

I took a deep breath and smiled back at her. "Yes, you still have a job. And apparently, another promotion as well." I reached across the table and took her hand. "I'm sorry for upsetting you. It was never my intention. I should have mentioned this to you in private before bringing it up like I did."

"It's okay," she smiled back at me. "I understand where you're coming from."

Jasmine returned to the table carrying a tray with our food and set each plate in front of us.

"Well, now that we have that all settled, let's eat," Paul exclaimed. Without another word, he dove into his food.

Chapter Fifteen

A shrill beeping rang through the early morning darkness and yanked me from a fitful sleep. I used to be excited about the new day as soon as I woke up, but over the course of the last two months of working construction my excitement faded more and more with each passing day. My quarter of a century long routine of waking up and painting something new and beautiful every day was replaced with waking up and going to a menial, monotonous job.

It also seemed that now I had more time to think about things. I had an hour drive to work, an hour return trip, and every night at home alone. The pattern formed early on. My thoughts during the drive to work in the morning cycled through whatever my dream the previous night had been— when I actually did have one. The drive home reminded me that I was heading home to an empty house. Then once I got home, my thoughts remained on the solitude of what was now my home.

I hurried through breakfast and got in my car to head north

to Charleston for another day at the job site. I was unable to shake the images of the dream I had the night before, the one that had been plaguing me for the past few weeks. I contemplated the dream while making the morning drive. On the surface, I knew that it had roots in the recent decision I made to keep the shop open, along with the approaching date of our anniversary. Even though the deeper meaning eluded me, I was not going to be discouraged from seeking the hidden meaning. To complicate matters further, the dream was an actual event that happened to me many years ago.

*   *   *

On our fifth wedding anniversary, Rebecca and I snuck off for the weekend to Edisto. Our small two-bedroom apartment in Wilmington had grown quite claustrophobic. My studio took up the entire second bedroom and left little room for anything else. There was a living room, a small kitchen, and an alcove set up as a dining area. That was the extent of the apartment, quaint and cozy but far too small. Maybe if I had a studio somewhere other than the apartment there wouldn't have been an issue with space, but that cost more money than we had to spare.

Rebecca took off Friday and Monday from her job as a sales clerk for Sears to make a long weekend. We drove down to the island on Thursday evening after she got home. The sun set a little more than halfway through the drive, just as we reached the northern end of the Francis Marion National Forest. The disappearance of the shimmering orange ball pulled the blanket of darkness over us from beyond the horizon.

I was alone with my thoughts. Rebecca had fallen asleep hours earlier as she always did on long drives. Images of the cottage flashed through my mind as I drove. The first time I visited it was back in our sophomore year of high school, some six months after we began dating. I joined Rebecca and her family for the week of Spring Break. It was a great trip, even though I spent the whole week sleeping on the lumpy and malformed couch. And I wouldn't have changed any of it for the world.

The faded gray clapboard structure sat nestled in a small grove of trees just north of Edisto Beach State Park, overlooking one of the many rivers and tributaries. The interior of the house now was exactly the same as it had been then and looked like it came straight out of the sixties, which added to the charm of the place. The large porch jutted out from the front of the house. The surrounding trees gave the lot an isolated feel, total seclusion from any neighbors.

It had been my idea to head to the cottage for our anniversary since it was also the spot where I first told Rebecca that I loved her back during our Spring Break trip. I couldn't think of a better place to spend our anniversary than where I first professed my love for her.

By the time we reached the island and pulled into the driveway it was just after ten at night. The soft chirping of crickets and other evening insects filled the night air as we made our way inside the cozy, two-bedroom house.

"It's been too long since we've been down here," Rebecca said.

"I know, especially since your parents hardly ever use the place. We should start coming more often."

We both agreed that it seemed to be a good idea at the moment, but I doubted whether we would follow through on it. I shrugged it off and carried our bags inside the cottage.

I woke up the next morning to the quiet chirping of birds

outside the window and felt more refreshed than I had in months. Rebecca was already awake and out of bed when I rolled over. I meandered through the cottage looking for her and found her sitting out on the porch sipping from a cup of coffee while reading a book. I leaned down and kissed her on the cheek before going back inside to the small kitchen.

The fifth anniversary seemed like a momentous occasion to me, second only to our first anniversary, so I decided to surprise Rebecca by cooking her breakfast. When I backed through the front door with two plates in my hand, Rebecca was still sitting on the porch where I found her a few minutes earlier. She looked up at me as I stepped toward the table with a huge smile on my face and carrying the still steaming breakfast.

"You didn't have to fix breakfast for me," she smiled as she took one of the plates from my outstretched hand.

"It's not a problem. I like doing things for you. Besides, it's our anniversary and you're not going to have to lift a finger to do anything."

Rebecca smiled as she rolled her eyes. She stuck her tongue out at me then picked up a crisp piece of bacon from the plate.

"So was there anything you wanted to do today?" I continued after taking a couple of bites.

"I would like to go over to Beaufort and walk through the shops and stores downtown."

"Sounds good to me. You want to go after breakfast? Then you can get your window-shopping and browsing time in."

Rebecca's head turned toward me. Her eyebrow arched upward. "Excuse me?"

I pressed my lips together with my lower lip jutting out as I shrugged my shoulders. "What?"

"You're actually going to go with me as I walk through the stores and shop for a couple hours? You don't even like going shopping when you need clothes for yourself."

"Well, it is our anniversary, so I can deal with it for one day and not complain. It is for you, after all."

"Okay, let me get this straight…" She repeated the question with sarcasm oozing from her voice. "You're actually going to go with me as I walk through the stores and shop for a couple hours?"

A smirk came to my face as I narrowed both eyes at her. "If you keep questioning me, I'll just head over to the beach and sit on one of the dunes while you shop."

Rebecca matched my smug expression. "I wouldn't advise that, not unless you want to spend our anniversary sleeping on the couch."

I dropped my chin and lowered my eyes in feigned defeat.

Rebecca grinned at me and pulled a small folded-up piece of paper from the front of the book. "Here, this might cheer you up."

I took the paper from her and unfolded it, running my hand along the folds to flatten the paper out. I read over each hand-written line.

A Wife's Prayer

Together we will live
Souls united from the start
From now until forever
I'll love you with all my heart
How we were brought together
God only knows
I'll be beside you always
Every time the soft breeze blows
Together we will live

In harmony and love
Blessed by what I've found
Sent from heaven above
As the days pass by
I will wait and pray
I'll be your strength
To help you through your day

I pulled my eyes away from the paper and looked up at Rebecca. "It's so beautiful. I love it." I leaned across the table and kissed her.

"Well, I've been trying to write the perfect piece for you for so long."

"You didn't have to do that. But I'm glad you did."

When we finished breakfast, I took the plates into the kitchen and washed them while Rebecca got ready. From the cottage, it was a little more than an hour's drive from Edisto to Beaufort. I had been there a few times before, but the true beauty of the quaint town always amazed me. The sweet smell of the lush marshland permeated the air as we crossed over the several bridges leading into town. I parked in the nearest open spot and climbed out of the car, pausing in the middle of the street to absorb the scenery. Rebecca got out and pulled me toward the sidewalk. We walked hand in hand along the store-fronts, half-staring at the shops and half-gazing out over the water at the end of the road. Nearly an hour and a half of shopping and walking passed by quickly. As it neared noon, we decided to stop at one of the local shops to eat lunch.

"What are you thinking about?" I stared into Rebecca's eyes, which were locked on the traffic outside the window.

"Oh, I don't know. Just that this place is so perfect. We should come down here more often, definitely more than once every couple of years."

"Then why don't we just move here?" I replied with a sarcastic playfulness.

"You'd get no complaints from me about that."

I looked over at Rebecca as her eyes rose to meet mine. "Are you serious? Do you really want to move here?"

"I'm serious. Just think of it. We could get out of our apartment and find a house. Until then, we could stay in my parent's cottage. This entire area is so beautiful. It would give you a whole new assortment of subjects to paint."

"But what about your job? There's no Sears down here for you to transfer to."

"I could find a new job. Or just start my own business. I mean, I did go to college for Business Administration. So it wouldn't be too hard to manage my own business. I'd just need to determine the market around here."

"So you're going to start your own store? Okay, then what are you going to sell?"

Rebecca stared at me with a single eyebrow raised. "Well, for starters, your paintings." Her face lit up. "Hey, that's what the store could be, an outlet for local artists and souvenirs."

"You think there would really be a big enough market for that?"

"Sure, why not? You've seen how popular your paintings are in Wilmington. Why wouldn't they be as popular here? If you ask me, the scenery is much better than back home, plus you'd have all the tourism. That would open up a new market for you."

"Exactly how long have you been thinking about this?"

"About maybe moving? I don't know, a couple of weeks. About moving here? In the five minutes since you mentioned it."

My eyebrow arched upward. "And in those five minutes you came up with this whole plan?"

She shrugged at me. "Hey, that's just how my mind works, I guess." Her gaze began to wander out the windows. She jumped up from the table and darted across the street. I jumped up and chased after her. She stopped in front of a boarded-up two-story building in the process of being renovated. "Right here. This would be the perfect spot for a store. It's right in the downtown area near the shopping and restaurants. Can't you just imagine it?"

I couldn't believe how much Rebecca was into the idea. I figured that when she saw just how much work was involved she would become more realistic about it. "If you want, why don't we see about coming back tomorrow to look at the place?"

"Really? You mean it?" She wrapped her arms around my neck and hugged me tightly, throwing me off balance. We crashed into the doorframe.

"Of course, if you really want to," I answered as I led her back toward the table where our lunch was waiting.

We finished eating, and then continued our wandering through the downtown shops of Beaufort. It was nearly dinner time when we returned to the cottage. We both cleaned up and drove over to Edisto Beach for a nice evening out followed by a moonlit walk on the beach. Exhausted when we returned for the night, we managed to crawl into bed and curl up next to each other only to fall asleep in each other's arms a few minutes later.

The morning came early with the sound of soft chirping outside of the bedroom window. I awoke to find Rebecca with her arms wrapped around me and her face inches in front of my own. I whispered a good morning to which she responded with a smile and leaned in to press her lips against mine. We continued to lay there in each other's arms as we welcomed the day.

Rebecca brought up walking through the renovated shop. I knew then that I would have to follow through on my promise made earlier and spent much of the next hour on the phone with a couple of different real estate offices. Once I tracked down the proper agent, I scheduled an appointment at the building for later that afternoon. Rebecca was overjoyed when I told her about the meeting. She jumped up and down all over the kitchen. It took a while, but I managed to settle her down enough to eat breakfast.

Since the restaurant was right across from the building, I decided that it would be just as convenient to eat lunch there again before the meeting. As soon as we finished, we walked across the street. The real estate agent hadn't arrived yet so Rebecca tried the door on a whim and found it was unlocked. She eased it open and poked her head through, calling out a loud greeting to anyone in the building. When there was no response, she pushed farther through the door. I followed her in and looked around the gutted interior. Makeshift sawhorses and benches were set up at various spots in the middle of the floor. A small, L-shaped staircase ran along the side wall toward the back of the room, but the steps themselves were missing.

I scraped my toe through a pile of dust on the floor, revealing faded hardwood floors. It occurred to me that with a little work and a lot of stain, the floors could once again shine.

"This place could be perfect. Don't you think?" I heard Rebecca ask, interrupting my train of thought.

"It is," I answered, and then muttered under my breath, "sure surprised me."

"What did you say?"

Before I was able to answer, the front door opened and the real estate agent stepped through the doorway. Her round, olive-toned face barely peaked through her mane of curly black hair. Once she saw us, she bounded across the room with her hand extended.

"Y'all must be the Banks'," she exclaimed, her face covered with the largest, toothiest smile I'd ever seen. "I'm Mattie Genero. I apologize if I'm late. The construction areas 'round here always confuse me. You'd think that after a year of it, I'd have it all figured out."

"It's not a problem," I said. "We got here early and the door was open so we decided to come on in."

Still smiling at us, she set her purse and briefcase on one of the makeshift tables. "So, did y'all get a chance to look around?" she asked as she rifled through a stack of papers from the briefcase.

"Yes, it's a beautiful building."

"And it's definitely got character," Rebecca added from behind me. "I can tell there must be a lot of interest in this space."

"To be honest, there is a lot of interest, but the construction is hindering any potential sale. Seems no one wants to wait 'til it's done. They want to get in immediately. It's a tad bit frustrating, if y'all know what I mean." I raised my eyebrows and she added more to her thought. "But don't get me wrong. This is still a prime spot with a great location. A hidden gem, in my humble opinion."

Mattie's demeanor relaxed a little as Rebecca grabbed my

arm and pulled me toward the side of the room. A huge grin spread across her face. She dragged me past the makeshift tables and stopped in a large open area, holding onto me as we spun around in a circle.

"Look at this place. Can't you just imagine how it would be once I got it all set up?" She pointed over by the staircase. "The register could go right there in the corner under the stairs. Have it on a corner desk with a little candy jar for the kids."

Seeing how it made her so happy to fantasize about the layout, I fell into step. "What about over there?" I pointed to the front corner next to the door where there was a large bowed-out window above a little ledge.

"Oh, right there? That's where all your paintings will go on little stands, or baby easels. That side of the front is going to be your own gallery. The other side will be a display area for other artists and featured items."

"My own personal window-front gallery?" On that suggestion, I started to rally to her idea. It really didn't seem too bad, considering she was making it up as she went along. "I could handle that. But do you think that there's going to be an interest in my work here?"

"Of course there will be, baby. People would be stupid not to have an interest in your work. Besides, with all the tourism around here, you couldn't ask for a better area."

"Yeah, but you have to say that. You're my wife. That makes you biased."

Rebecca shot a slanted glance at me, her lips pressed together. "Maybe so, but it doesn't make me any less right."

I reached out and pulled her close to me.

She looked up at me and the corners of her lips curved upward. "Yeah, you better try to make up for your last comment."

I leaned down and pressed my lips to hers. Her arms draped around my neck as she kissed me back. Lost in our embrace, we barely heard the quiet ruffling of papers from across the room. I pulled back as Rebecca released my neck. Mattie was still standing at the makeshift table, attempting to be unobtrusive as she allowed us to look around and talk.

"So sorry about that. I didn't mean to interrupt."

"No, it's okay," I responded. "We didn't mean to ignore you."

A bright smile flashed on Mattie's face as she walked toward us. Though we had already walked around the entire first floor, she still led us around and went through a mental list of key points. We ended up back at the makeshift table. "So what do y'all think of the place? It's certainly a special little spot."

"We won't argue with you there," I agreed. "Do you have any information that we could take with us and look over? We aren't in a position to make any decisions right now, but we will look over the info and talk about it. We'll get back to you soon, if that's okay."

"Of course, dear, that's perfectly fine." Mattie pulled out a small folder from her briefcase and removed a stapled packet of paper from it.

I took the packet from her hand and flipped through it. "Thanks. We will look over this and call you sometime next week, once we get back home from vacation."

"Sounds perfect," she responded as she closed up her briefcase and extended her hand to us. "T'was a pleasure to meet you, too. I'll look forward to hearing from y'all next week."

Both Rebecca and I shook Mattie's hand and made our way

toward the front door. We stepped out into the bright, cloud-less afternoon. Mattie followed us out and locked the door be-hind us. We all exchanged another quick goodbye before Mattie walked off down the sidewalk. Rebecca and I remained behind and looked around the immediate area. In the past day, the area had already started to grow on me. It seemed like a nice place to be able to call home.

* * *

I came to the conclusion that I had the same dream of our fifth anniversary because our anniversary would have been in two weeks if she were still alive. I will still celebrate it, even if I spend the whole evening alone sitting beside her gravesite.

Throughout the entire day at work, I couldn't shake the memory. It stayed in the forefront of my thoughts the entire time and made work somewhat difficult. The day ended after what seemed like an eternity and I drove home, but the change of location had no bearing on the situation as my thoughts re-mained on the dream, and the dream alone.

Chapter Sixteen

In the nearly three months since Rebecca died I'd only left the house a handful of times outside of going to work and had little to no contact with anyone other than my coworkers. Every little thing around the house, however insignificant, reminded me of my wife. Every object had a meaning, a story that flooded back into my mind when I saw it. I spent all my time sitting in the darkened house for fear of seeing something that triggered an all-consuming memory. The couch had conformed around my body so much that even when I wasn't sitting down, I could see the contours of my form in the cushions.

Every night I stared at the television for hours on end with remote in hand, watching the bright screen as it cast long shadows across the walls. This time I watched a grainy video playing back on the screen, replaying the events of Cheryl's first birthday. It happened nearly sixteen years ago, but I remembered it as if it were last week.

Cheryl's birthday was in early March. It had been a beautiful and, for a change, warm period that year. Mark and Kelly decided to take a long weekend and drove down to celebrate at our house. That Christmas, I had received a new camcorder and was stuck in the 'filming everything in sight' phase. So it came as no surprise when I pulled out the camera to film the party. We decided to have the party outside, the first cookout of the new year. Cheryl had just learned to walk about a week before her birthday and spent the better part of the party wobbling around the yard with Rebecca chasing a few feet behind. Kelly and Mark sat at the picnic table watching. A few weeks earlier, they found out that Kelly was pregnant with their second child so the party served as a double event, Cheryl's birthday and the pregnancy celebration. The camera paused on Mark and Kelly and then zoomed in far too close. I heard myself talking from behind the camera.

"Hey, you two."

They both looked up at the camera and smiled. Kelly waved as I circled around them filming from every angle.

"Having fun yet?"

"Of course," Kelly answered. "Are you having fun filming everything?"

"I can't believe you even had to ask me that," I retorted. "Hey, Mark, how's the food coming?"

"I just threw the burgers on a few minutes ago, so I guess it's about time to flip them."

The camera zoomed in closer on the two of them. "Well, maybe if you stopped necking with your wife for a minute, we could finally have some food to eat."

Kelly shot a sneering glare at me through the camera and Mark pretended like he was about to stand up. I hurried away toward Rebecca and Cheryl, who were playing down in the sand. I snuck up behind the two of them as they sat on the beach.

"Hey Bec. Smile. You're on TV."

She turned toward me and smiled. The light breeze whisked through her hair, sending it in waves behind her. She held Cheryl and pointed up at the camera, getting Cheryl to notice me as I stood above them. Cheryl started to squirm around when she saw me. Rebecca tried to calm her down and played with her, making her wave to the camera.

"Are you trying to turn me into a movie star?"

"Not a chance. Then I would have tons of guys trying to steal you away from me."

Rebecca tilted her head to the side and scrunched her eyebrows together. "You don't ever have to worry about that. Now put that camera down and get over here."

I set the camera down on a bench, but apparently forgot to stop recording. The camera still captured footage as I walked around and sat down with Rebecca and Cheryl. I rubbed Cheryl's head and gave Rebecca a kiss. When our lips parted, she looked deep into my eyes as if she were completely caught up in the moment.

"So is it done yet?"

My head pulled back and I just stared over at her. "Excuse me?"

"The food," she said. "Is it done yet?"

"Oh, not yet. Mark said it would be done soon."

The corners of her lips arched downward in disappointment. "You promised me that it would be finished before my parents got here."

"And it will be," I assured her. "It's almost finished and they aren't here yet."

"Well, they will be here soon."

I leaned in to kiss her again, this time on her forehead. "Don't worry, it'll be ready. I promise." I hopped up from the sand and grabbed the camera off of the bench to resume film- ing the events. I focused the camera on Rebecca. Her nose scrunched up as she shot me a playful sneer.

"Stop playing with that camera and go fix the food."

"Yes, master."

The sneer melted from her face, replaced by a flirtatious smile. "Now that's more like it."

The focus on the screen dropped from Rebecca's face to the sand before cutting off to a black screen. I continued to sit there, staring at the blank screen for a few minutes. The words from the video echoed through my mind: You promised me that it would be finished. I just couldn't shake that phrase. As my eyes closed, the unfinished portrait flashed in my mind's eye and I realized why that phrase was stuck in my head.

I pushed myself to my feet and walked down the hall. My destination was clear. The short journey ended in front of the closed studio door. My hand reached out for the knob. The metal felt cool against my skin as I turned the knob. Nervous- ness, anxiety, and fear washed over me. The thought of what was on the other side of the door, although I knew exactly what it was, terrified me. My hand jerked away from the knob and I backed away from the door. I was torn between fear of what waited for me on the other side and disappointment that I couldn't open the door. A strange comfort in knowing that the door would still be there tomorrow if I wanted to try again worked up from the depths of my soul.

* * *

A shrill squawking of a laughing gull outside my window pulled me out of a restless sleep. I woke up confused, vaguely remembering bits and pieces of a dream, but not quite sure what happened in it. All I remembered was walking toward a goal but never reaching it. I could get close but never close enough. What the prize had been remained a mystery, so close, yet just out of reach. That gap could never be bridged because I couldn't concentrate with the racket taking place outside my window.

I threw aside the covers and climbed out of bed. Three laughing gulls sat perched on the sand dune near my window. Two of them began to fight over an unseen treasure, squawking and pecking as the third sat back watching. I pounded my fist against the window, gaining the birds' attention as their shrill cries pierced the quiet of the morning. They stood in place on the dune and stared back at me. I swore those birds knew what they were doing. In a retaliatory action, I sneered back at them and pounded the window again. They took flight and soared through the air, landing on a nearby dune farther down the beach. As long as they weren't near me and I couldn't hear them, I didn't really care where they went.

When I walked out of the bedroom, I paused in the hall as my eye caught the shadow of the studio door. Again, I stopped in front of the closed door and reached out for the knob. The cool sensation of the metal against my skin from the previous night was gone. I now felt the warmth of the knob against the palm of my hand as I turned it.

The door creaked open, hinges squeaking after nearly three months of disuse. I inched my body closer and closer until I moved over the threshold and into the room. A thin layer of dust covered everything, reflecting slivers of sunlight slipping through the partially drawn curtain. A musty, stale odor wafted into my nostrils. I pulled back the curtains and opened the windows to air out the room. The bright sunlight filtered in, blinding me. I blindly reached up for the thin chain on the fan. A cool wave of fresh air filled the room as the blades increased in speed.

My gaze paused on the easel in the corner of the room by the table. The half-finished image staring back at me was the same image that had been haunting my dreams at night and my thoughts during the day. I remained fixated on the canvas. My eyes focused on the blue acrylic eyes of my wife, so vivid, so lifelike. My grip on reality quickly faded into a blur as they drew me in, pulling me closer. My hand reached out toward the canvas. The familiar rough texture of the taut cloth felt like silk against my fingertips. I looked down to the table where my brushes were lined up in a row with tubes of paint in color order beside them, just how I left them so long ago.

Two small pictures in a double glass frame sat on the shelf above the table. I reached up and removed the frame from the shelf. I wiped the thin layer of dust covering the glass with my sleeve and stared at it. The picture in the left frame was from before dinner the night I proposed to her and the picture on the right was from our wedding. I replaced the frame on the shelf as the memory of the night I proposed played in my mind. So much work and effort was put into making that night as perfect as possible.

* * *

The ten hour drive home passed with excruciating slowness. I had just graduated from NYU's Steinhardt School of Education. My ideal plan was to leave the day after graduation, but last minute events such as packing and saying my goodbyes to friends prevented that. There was also only one thing on my mind that made it hard to focus: Rebecca.

The majority of the drive home passed by subconsciously as the next thing I knew, I was pulling into the driveway at my parents' house. I grabbed a few bags and carried them inside.

My dad hurried down the stairs and followed me to help with the unloading. A few more trips back to the car and we were finished. Once the last bag hit the floor in the hallway, I hurried to the kitchen where my mom was fixing dinner. I wrapped my arms around her from behind and kissed her on the cheek.

"Hey, Momma."

"Hey, baby," she smiled back at me, kissing my cheek in return. Her eyes locked onto mine and she answered my question before I could even ask it. "Don't worry about it. We took care of everything. All you have to do is pick her up and show up at the restaurant."

"Thanks, Momma." I hugged her again. "I wouldn't have been able to do this without all your help."

"Well, that's what I'm here for."

All of the plans for the evening had already been set up prior to my leaving New York. I had enlisted the help of my parents when they came up for my graduation. They were thrilled with my 'secret plan'—I called it a secret plan because most of the planning took place while Rebecca was in the other room of my apartment after the graduation ceremony. I knew that I wouldn't have been able to pull it off without my parents' help. They were the ones who made the dinner reservations and coordinated everything with the restaurant staff. All I had to do was be at the designated place at the appointed time.

It was a little before seven when I pulled out of the driveway to make my way to Rebecca's. With a quick wave to my parents, I backed out of the driveway and sped off down the road. Rebecca lived less than ten minutes from my house and the restaurant was only a few miles from hers, so I knew I had plenty of time to make our seven-thirty reservation.

I arrived at her house and parked my black, '64 Ford Thunderbird behind her dad's station wagon. I hurried up the sidewalk and rang the doorbell. Rebecca's dad, Richard, opened the door a few seconds later.

"Hey, Martin," he greeted me with a smile and extended out his hand. "How was the drive back?"

"Long, as usual," I answered, barely able to shake his hand before he ushered me toward the living room. "But it's definitely worth it to finally be back home."

"I can imagine. Rebecca will be down in a second. You know how girls are, always primping."

We sat in silence for a few minutes. Mr. Billings already knew what I was planning to do that night. When I came home for Easter break a little more than a month earlier, I stopped by when Rebecca wasn't home and asked his permission. He gave his blessing and said it was a long time coming but that he was glad it was going to happen. I had always thought of the Billings family as an extension of my own family, ever since the first time I met them just after Rebecca and I began dating.

Mr. Billings leaned closer to me and spoke in a hushed whisper. "Is everything ready?"

Before I could answer, there came a squeak from the top of the steps as Rebecca began her descent to join us. I just nodded quickly to answer his question.

Her dad leaned back and brought up a new subject. "I'm sorry we couldn't make it up for graduation. I just didn't have the vacation days. Did you get the gift we sent with Becca?"

"I did. Thank you so much. I'm still working on all the

thank-you cards. Hopefully, I'll finish them up in a few days."

"Well, it was our pleasure. You know we've always loved having you around the past, oh, seven years, even if you were up in New York for the last four of them."

"Wow, has it really been that long, Daddy?" Rebecca slipped into the room behind us. "We had no idea. I'm glad you've been keeping track of the time."

Her father and I both stood and turned toward Rebecca. My jaw dropped. She wore a long blue, satiny, sleeveless dress the same color as her eyes. Her hair was pulled back. Two single braids traced their way along either side of her head, forming a crown, before joining together in a single braid and draping down her back. Rebecca appeared to glide across the room toward me. Her walk was graceful, yet absolutely seductive, very much like the day we met seven years earlier. When I told her about taking her out to dinner when I got home, I mentioned it was a nice restaurant and figured she would be dressed up, but I didn't know she would look so beautiful. I managed to pry my eyes away from her and glanced down at my own clothes. I suddenly felt underdressed as I stood there in tan slacks, a blue shirt and black tie.

"So how do I look?" she asked, batting her big, baby blue eyes at me. Her perfect smile beamed at me, making me melt and lose my train of thought.

"You look absolutely amazing," I stammered, pulling her into a quick embrace with a brief kiss on her cheek.

We separated from our hug and stood there. Without understanding how it was possible, her smile seemed to grow even wider and more brilliant as I commented on her appearance. Mr. Billings stepped in and slipped his arm around Rebecca.

"You two have fun tonight," he said as he kissed Rebecca on the cheek. We all walked to the door where he winked at me and smiled. "Don't keep her out too late. I wouldn't want to have to send the deputies out after you two."

"Don't worry," I played along. "I'll have her back early."

Rebecca slipped her arm through mine as we stepped out on the porch and into the breezy evening. I opened the car door and she slipped into the passenger seat then I hurried around and slid behind the wheel. With a turn of the key, the engine roared to life and we backed down the driveway and began the short drive to the restaurant.

We arrived at The Pilot House Restaurant a few minutes before our seven-thirty reservation. I parked the car and escorted Rebecca toward the yellow clapboard building. We walked arm in arm, looking out over the Cape Fear River as the sun slowly sank in the distance.

I stopped in front of the building to take in the historic surroundings, not wanting to forget a single detail of the special night. The building had been erected over one hundred years ago, but the restaurant had only opened a few years earlier in 1978. However, in those few short years, the reputation for excellent food and fine dining had grown throughout the community.

The path led past a line of small bushes, onto the porch edged with a white banister, then by two large white rocking chairs beside the front door. The host greeted us as we stepped inside and immediately led us to the table I had requested that overlooked the river. A moment later we were seated and a waiter took our drink order. Rebecca stared out over the water. The setting sun reflected on the rippling river. Every few minutes a small fishing boat would pass by, returning to port from a long day at sea. Several sailboats also passed by. Their white sails cut through the evening breeze as they made their way home.

"It's really beautiful, isn't it?"

A soft smile crossed her lips as her gaze shifted from the water back to me. "Very much so. I see sights like this all the time, but it still never ceases to amaze me with its beauty."

I gazed into her eyes, lost in the moment. My eyes never wavered from hers. "I know exactly how you feel."

The moment was perfect, as if all the planets and stars were in perfect alignment. I wanted to ask the question, but when I opened my mouth, there was only silence. No words came out. The perfect moment slipped away as we sat there. I spent the next twenty minutes kicking myself for freezing and wasting such a perfect opportunity.

"Is everything okay?" Rebecca asked me. She leaned forward and reached for my hand from across the table. Her fingertips caressed the back of my hand.

A small lump began to form in my throat. I wanted to ask her the question I had waited so long for, but I held back. The perfect moment had already passed and I would simply have to wait for another opportunity to present itself.

"I'm fine. Why do you ask?"

"You seem a little distracted. That's all." Her blue eyes seemed to pierce right through me as if she knew I was hiding something.

"Oh, it's nothing," I changed the subject but still managed to throw in a hint to her. "I'll tell you about it later. I promise."

"If you say so, dear." Her expression was smug. I could tell that she was a little let down that I didn't talk about it then. My mind raced through various other topics to talk about before coming to one that could work.

"How were your finals?" Rebecca's finals started earlier that week. I knew how important they were with her graduation only a few days away, yet somehow she still managed to come up the previous weekend for my graduation. And it also worked out that the following day was the only day the whole week she didn't have a final, so she was able to go out without having to worry about her studies.

Rebecca paused for a second before answering. "They were all right. The only two I was worried about were on Monday and Tuesday. I've got my last two on Friday, but I'm not worried about either of them."

"Well, I know I said it before, but I'll say it again. I'm really glad you came up for graduation. I know you could have stayed here and studied instead."

"Oh, you know that I wouldn't have missed it for the world."

I was amazed at how fast the perfect moment came again as I smiled at her. This time, under my own discretion, I held off popping the question. A rather impulsive idea popped into my head. I decided that I would wait until after dinner and take Rebecca for a walk along the docks. It would be there that I would ask her.

The waiter approached the table with our meals. It was funny because I didn't even remember ordering in the first place. He set the two plates of food down in front of us then slowly backed away. The aroma of the freshly prepared food wafted toward my nostrils. Rebecca had ordered the Roasted Red Pepper Chicken. Her dinner looked positively appetizing with the chicken and peppers resting on a bed of linguini along with sautéed mushrooms. My gaze drifted down to my own meal, the Shrimp and Crawfish Etouffe. I had always enjoyed spicy foods, though it was not a trait that Rebecca shared. As I looked down at my plate, it occurred to me that maybe spicy wasn't an appropriate meal for tonight, with the importance of the evening.

"Wow, this looks delicious," Rebecca said, leaning forward and inhaling. Her eyes closed as the scent of the chicken washed over her face.

From across the table, I watched her pierce the chicken then slice off a small sliver and twist the fork in the linguini. Once the noodles were wound in a tight roll around the chicken on the fork, she raised it to her mouth. A series of flavor explosions consumed her face with each bite.

"Looks like it tastes as good as it smells, doesn't it?" As I waited for her answer, I took my first taste of my shrimp. Biting down released a sudden surge of warmth and spices that overwhelmed my taste buds. The extreme flavor sensation caused my eyes to water. I dropped the fork on the plate and dabbed my tearing eyes with the napkin before gulping down half of the glass of water in front of me, which only served to spread the fire in my mouth.

Rebecca put her fork down and looked over at me, half concerned and half amused at my predicament. "Are you going to be okay?"

"I sure hope so. I just wasn't expecting it to be that spicy." My vision blurred through watery eyes. I coughed to try to clear my scratchy throat, while trying not to disturb any of the other couples seated around us. I wiped my eyes one last time and took a sip of water before repeating my question. "So, we all know how my food is, but does yours taste as good as it smells?"

"Definitely. This is easily one of the best meals I've ever tasted." Rebecca cut off another bite of her chicken and skewered a mushroom with her fork.

I smiled as her eyes closed, savoring the flavor. As her eyes opened, the smile vanished from my face. I couldn't let her know everything that was going on in my head. Some things had to be left as an unfolding mystery, residing just under the surface, waiting to be discovered.

I glanced down at my plate and decided to brave another bite of the shrimp. This time I was prepared for the spicy flavor and was determined not to let it overpower me as with the last bite. After spearing the next shrimp with the fork, the small, crescent-shaped piece of meat glared back at me as I raised the fork toward my mouth.

Rebecca grinned as she watched me as I stared at my fork. "Aw, are you scared of the itty-bitty shrimp? It won't bite back. I promise."

My eyes narrowed, glaring playfully back at her. In spite of my careful setup, I bit down on the shrimp, chewing, and then swallowing as fast as possible to not give the spices a chance to torture my taste buds again. With my mouth empty, I grinned at her in playful victory. "I showed that shrimp who was boss."

"You're my hero. I don't know what I would do without you here to protect me from the vast army of invading shrimp."

I leaned back in my chair with an air of embattled victory about me. "Well, it was my pleasure, m'lady. No ill will shall befall you during my watch, which will hopefully be for a long time to come."

Rebecca tilted her head and arched her eyebrow at me. I held my breath, hoping the comment would pass without any further discussion, but I knew that was too much to ask for. All I could do was to offer up a distracting comment.

"So what time do we need to be there for graduation?"

The questioning look on her face relaxed and her arched eyebrow returned to normal. A smile peeked through her pursed lips. "The ceremony starts at noon. My parents said they were getting there around eleven, so they will save you seats."

"That works for me," I smiled back at her, silently congratulating myself on avoiding the topic, at least for the time being.

We smiled longingly at each other and continued eating. Before we knew it, an hour had passed by. Both of us had long since finished our dinner but had remained deep in conversation, aided by several refills of sweet tea. At some point in the discussion of a gallery showing in New York that I had as part of my senior portfolio, I happened to glance down at my watch and noticed it was just past nine. Not wanting to cut anything short, I tried to think of ways to ease into a transition toward the door.

"How was the chicken?" I asked, glancing down at her empty plate.

"It was amazing." Her hand drifted down to her stomach. "How was yours?"

"Very good, once I got over the initial spiciness." I grinned at her across the table and she smiled back. "Do you want anything else? Dessert?"

Rebecca's eyebrows scrunched together as she exhaled. "I would love it, but I'm already stuffed." Her focus shifted up to my face. "But don't let that stop you from getting it if you want."

I shook my head, pressing my lips together. "No, I'm

good," I answered with a casual wave of my hand. "You ready to get out of here?"

Rebecca nodded at me as a small smile escaped through her lips. I raised my hand to signal the waiter to bring the check. We walked out of the restaurant a few minutes later. As we passed the two white rocking chairs on the porch, Rebecca slipped her arm through mine. The dark, cloudless sky was dotted with tiny specks of stars, visible once we stepped off of the porch.

I paused halfway to the car and turned to face Rebecca. "Do you want to go for a walk before we leave?"

The gentle evening breeze blew in from the river, tossing her hair across her face. She reached up and pulled back a few strands of hair, tucking them behind her ear as she answered. "I'd love to."

We walked down the street and past Milton's Market. Beside the market there was a small alleyway that led around behind the building to a little pier. The air was musty and smelled of fish, which didn't set the mood the way I had hoped. But by the time we reached the pier the odor of fish had waned. The air was now filled with the scent of the rushing evening river and the marshland from the opposite bank of the water. At the end of the pier was a small, rickety wooden bench. It looked as if it had been hand crafted by one of the various shipping captains that passed through Wilmington over a hundred years ago. Rebecca sat right down on the bench and looked out over the water. The moon shone high above us, spreading its pale light over the rushing water. I was hesitant to sit on the bench, not wanting the thing to give out on us, so I leaned against the railing next to her. Where I stood or sat was of no concern to me anyway, since I would be down on my knee in a few minutes, if all went right.

"I never want to live anywhere farther than a stone's throw from the water," Rebecca stated, her eyes never leaving the river. "It's so peaceful and refreshing. Don't you think?"

"Of course, I can never picture myself living anywhere else, either. I tried living up in New York for school and I couldn't wait to get back here."

"I couldn't wait for you to get back, either. You have no idea how much I missed you when you were gone."

"Oh, I think I have a pretty fair idea." Taking both of her hands in mine, I leaned down to give her a soft kiss. "All I could think about the entire time I was in New York was finishing up so I could get back here, back to you. I was left with just one solution. One question that I had to ask." I dropped to one knee and held her left hand, lowering my head to kiss her finger. My free hand slipped into my pocket and pulled out a small black velvet box. I opened the box to reveal a ring with a small, square-cut stone.

Rebecca's hand flew up and covered her mouth. I raised the open box up toward her. The moonlight glinted off of the sparkling stone.

"I've been dying to ask you all night. I know it's not a diamond and I promise I will get you a diamond eventually, but I thought you would like this."

"Oh, Martin, it's beautiful. It's a sapphire, my birth stone. That's even better than a diamond."

I slipped the ring onto the tip of her finger as I looked up at Rebecca. Tears streamed down her cheeks, leaving narrow trails that caught the rays of moonlight and left a faint glow about her face.

"Bec, I love you more than anything. I've known that since

the first time you walked past me. I've always wanted to love you, take care of you, and make you happy. You are the one person in the world that I want by my side." I had hoped to give her the beautiful, articulate proposal I had rehearsed so many times, but I couldn't hold it inside anymore. "Rebecca, will you marry me?"

With tears streaming, the small smile that had been on Rebecca's lips since I sank to my knee was replaced by an enormous beaming smile. She nodded her head vigorously as she took several deep breaths. Her eyes closed for a second as she exhaled. "Yes, yes, I'll marry you," she whispered.

I slid the ring onto her finger, gently coaxing it past her knuckle. With extreme carefulness, I eased down on the bench next to her. My hand drifted up to her face and tucked a few strands of wind-tossed hair behind her ear. I caressed her cheek with the back of my fingers and wiped the tears away before I leaned over and touched my lips to hers. The kiss seemed to last an eternity. Her hands clasped the side of my face, holding me closer to her. Our lips separated, but our heads remained only a few inches apart as we gazed into each other's eyes, losing all track of time.

The shrill horn of a passing trawler snapped us out of our engaging trance. I paused to look down at my watch, shocked to notice what time it was. The look must have been evident on my face as well, because Rebecca questioned me about it.

"What is it?"

"It's just after ten o'clock. I had no idea we were sitting out here for so long."

Rebecca smiled over at me. "Did you have big plans for the rest of the night? Another hot date you have to get to?"

"Nope," I answered. A witty comeback popped into my

head. "I only had one hot date tonight. And it just became one that will last the rest of my life."

Rebecca shook her head. "How long did you stay up last night thinking that line up?"

"Actually, I came up with it on the ten hour drive home. But I was up all last night trying to put into words exactly how I feel about you," I said, reaching into my pocket and removing a small folded-up piece of paper. "This was all I could come up with."

I handed her the paper. She unfolded it and held it up. The moon gave off just enough light for Rebecca to be able to read the handwritten lines on the page.

The Last Piece

Life is a complicated matter,
An intricate puzzle to fill.
Careers, hobbies and talents
Make for a myriad of skills
Through all my time,
Edges of my puzzle bound.
One piece was always missing,
Hidden, nowhere to be found.
I searched high and low,
But the piece remained lost.
All hope gone, goals unfinished,
The finish line far from crossed.
Then came a day long overdue,
The answer to my prayers.
A new wind blew fresh hope
A whole new set of cares.
Never thought the day would come
The final piece has shown true.
In the great puzzle that is me
This one last piece is you.

No sooner had she finished reading to herself than her eyes

once again welled up with tears. She looked over at me as the first tear escaped from her eye and carved a path down her cheek, dangling on her chin for a second before releasing.

"It's beautiful."

My arm slid around her shoulder and I pulled her closer to me. "Well, I'm no poet, but that's exactly how I feel and what you mean to me."

Rebecca leaned in and kissed me again before resting her head down on my shoulder. "You may think you're no poet, but that really was amazing. You should keep writing. I had no idea you could write like that."

I squeezed my arm around her and kissed the top of her head. "Well, I had a little help on this one. The perfect inspiration was running through my mind as I wrote it."

We sat there together on the bench for a few more minutes before walking along the pier back toward the street. Soon after, we were in the car and driving back to Rebecca's house. By my estimate, we would get to her house around a quarter to eleven. I just found it ironic that we were both about to be college graduates and were now engaged to be married, yet I still had her home fifteen minutes before her old high school curfew.

Just as I predicted, I pulled into the driveway at Rebecca's house at a quarter to eleven. The house was dark with the exception of the porch light that shone through the night. We walked to the door, hand in hand, and paused on the stoop long enough to get lost in each other's eyes once more. I leaned down to engage her in a brief goodnight kiss.

No sooner had our lips touched than the lock on the door was undone and the front door flew open. Much to our surprise, both sets of our parents along with Rebecca's younger sister, Kelly, were standing in the foyer. They all had enormous smiles on their faces as they beckoned us to come inside.

"Did you know about this?" Rebecca whispered to me as we stepped through the door.

"I had no idea," I answered under my breath. Mr. Billings closed the door behind us.

*　*　*

My eyes remained fixed on the glass frame, reflecting the spinning ceiling fan. As I sat hypnotized by the blades, the memory of the proposal night played through my mind for a second time. I broke free of the self-imposed trance and shifted around on the stool. The half-finished portrait once again dominated my field of view and I was unable to remove my eyes from it. The words from the video continued to echo through my mind: You promised me that it would be finished. Suddenly, I realized why I couldn't shake the phrase before. I promised Rebecca that I would finish her portrait no matter what. In the few months that have passed since then, I had been too blinded by grief, pain, or fear to fulfill that promise.

I now realized I had already taken the first steps to keeping my promise. After months of living in seclusion outside the locked door of the studio, I had now opened that door and stepped back into my previous world. Whether I was truly ready for that remained to be seen, but at least I was there.

But things must advance step by step, and this was no different. My first step was opening the door and setting foot inside the studio. The next step would be to pick up a brush and try to paint, but that challenge would be one left for another time as the emotions of being in the room began to overtake my senses.

I made a quick beeline for the door, trying to escape from

the emotional hold the room seemed to have over me. But unlike the last time I walked out of the room, this time I left the door unlocked and open behind me, welcoming my next visit.

Chapter Seventeen

Usually when people are confronted by something they fear they want to run away from it as fast as possible. They often don't try to overcome the hurdle for the simple fact that it terrifies them and, as a whole, people are afraid of failure. That was the exact situation I found myself in regarding the painting. All I had to do was decide which person I wanted to be: the person who ran away from fear or the person who stood up and confronted it. The answer became obvious in a second, but it was not so easy to implement. Because there were so many emotions involved with trying to finish the painting, I spent most of that morning sitting out on the jetty, staring at the small pool of calm water within the circle of rocks.

The sun burned down straight above me as I climbed across the jetty and strolled back toward the house. The time had come to stand up to my fears and continue the portrait, just like I promised. I hurried into the house and walked straight to the studio with a renewed enthusiasm. The realism of my actions began to set in as I stepped through the doorway. I paused and took another minute to look around the room, not believing that this morning was only the second time I had set foot in the studio in over three months. Prior to the past few months, the longest I had gone without painting in the last thirty-five years was a week at most, and that was when we had been on vacation. My gaze drifted around the room and I felt as if I was returning home after being gone for far too long.

I crossed the room and sat down at the easel. My hand reached out for the canvas. The painted surface felt smooth under my fingertips as I traced the visible brush strokes. I brushed against the ambiguous shape of Rebecca's face, the back of my finger sliding down her cheek. As I pulled away from the canvas, I noticed the trail my fingers had left through the thin film of dust covering the painting. A light puff of breath from the side of the canvas roused a small cloud that glinted in the afternoon light. I grabbed a small rag that sat balled up on the table and made my way to the bathroom. I held the rag under the cool, running water, then rung it out tightly. Returning to the easel, I wiped down the canvas with the damp rag until the painting gleamed in the light.

I retook my place on the stool and sat staring at the painting. Rebecca's cool, blue eyes gazed down in a thoughtful stare. Though her face still lacked the finished detail, the slight upward curve of her lips stood out in my mind, as if she was grateful that I was back in front of her. I kissed the tip of my index finger, and then pressed it over the outline of her lips.

"I'm sorry it's taken me so long to come back to you," I whispered. "When I lost you, I lost my focus, my reason for living. But that's back now. Somehow you reminded me of it, and here I am again."

My eyes glazed over with a thin film. I fluttered my eyelids and stared up at the ceiling, hoping to dissipate the tears. I turned away and wiped my eyes with my shirtsleeve. My attention focused on the table beside me. The brushes sat in a neat line just as I had left them. I reached out and grabbed one of the larger brushes. The bristles felt rigid to the touch after the long months of neglect, but they soon became soft and pliable in my fingers.

I set the brush back on the table next to the other brushes and picked up a tube of paint. The label read Cadmium Red Acrylic Paint. I twisted off the cap and raised the open tube to my nose. The smell of the paint filled my nostrils with a fragrance that had been absent for far too long. With a dab of the red paint onto the palette, a new phase of my life began. To the red I added the smallest trace of Titanium White to create a lavish pink shade to fill in Rebecca's lips. I spread the paint over the canvas with my finest tipped brush. It amazed me that the brush still felt like an extension of my own hand, even though I had taken so much time away from painting.

Rebecca's face slowly rose from the undefined pale white skin tone. Her lips were parted, allowing the faintest bit of white to be seen between them. Her figure drew me into a trance. I couldn't take my eyes off of her.

I cleaned off the fine brush and mixed more Titanium White into the pink glob of paint. With a little paint on the brush, I dabbed two small spots on each cheek, then took another fine dry brush and spread the dots out to add a bit of color to her cheeks. I worked my way down and added more and more detail to the once ambiguous painting. Burnt Umber and a few drops of white created the color for Rebecca's jaw line and the light shadows on her neck and shoulders. The rest of the color filled in the curves of her cleavage, just peaking out over the small V that made up the neckline.

The next area to fill in was the dress itself. Titanium White and Titan Buff swirled together to form the color of the silk, and then a drop of Burnt Umber was added to give tone and shadow. I brushed in the small arcs to define her bust line beneath the fabric. Searching through the brushes, I grabbed one with a tip no larger than a pencil point and began stroking in the small folds of the fabric that covered the legs that were curled beneath her.

All the shadows, highlights, and detail I added soon filled in Rebecca's figure. Her features stood out from the rest of the picture. I paused for a moment to admire her. Her sandy blonde hair flared out at the tips. Most was tucked loosely behind her ear, but a few strands hung along her cheek. The satiny white fabric of the dress clung to every curve of her body and accentuated her perfect figure before hanging over the front of the couch.

My attention moved to the rest of the painting, now glaringly lacking in detail. I mixed together some green with a dab of black and added color to the couch beneath Rebecca. More texture for the pale yellow wall nearly completed the painting.

A few strokes later, the ocean appeared outside the window with small breaking whitecaps and a trail of bubbling foam along the shoreline. Rinsing out the brush in a cup of water, the feeling kept nagging at me that there was still something missing, something very important and essential to the painting.

"I want the sun shining down on me through the open window." Rebecca's voice sounded clearly in my mind.

That was it. That's what was missing. Rebecca's words echoed through my mind again as I reached for the tubes of Cadmium Red and Yellow. I painted the sun only a few moments after sunrise. Sunrise and sunset had been our favorite times of the day because the sky seemed to explode with all of the different colors. I mixed the perfect tone and brushed in the sun peeking over the watery horizon.

I dropped the brush in the water and gazed back over the painting. Rebecca's figure looked stunning, perfect. There was just one more thing. It wasn't in the original sketch or there when Rebecca posed, but it was something I wanted to add for myself. I grabbed the fine-tipped brush and squeezed out a dab of Cadmium Red. Scattered petals of a red rose appeared to the left side of Rebecca's dress just below her shoulder. But it didn't stop there. I painted four long-stemmed roses resting on her lap.

"Now," I whispered, "now the painting is finally complete." After so long, I wasn't quite sure how to feel, or what to think. I dropped the palette on the table and left the brushes as they were. My chin fell into my hands and I sat staring at the painting.

I pulled myself out of the daze that had held me captivated for over an hour. My cheeks were puffy and moist. I realized that I had been crying. I wiped my eyes with the back of my hand and readjusted my position on the stool. Everything in the room blurred into ambiguity with the exception of the painting. My hand reached out toward the canvas, my finger tips running down Rebecca's lifelike cheek.

"I miss you so much. It's so hard not having you here with me. I don't know if I can keep this up for much longer."

My emotions began to overwhelm me once again. The tears welled up and carved parallel routes down my cheeks. I moved over to the table to straighten up, cleaning the used brushes out in a cup of water. Two tubes of paint were still open. I grabbed one of them and held it up to my face, again breathing in the fragrance from the open container. My eyes clenched shut, forcing out the lingering tears. They raced down my cheek and paused for a second on my jaw before releasing and plunging headlong into the open containers as I took one more deep breath of their scent. I closed the lids to the paints and crossed the room to the window.

The evening sun had long since disappeared behind the house. A black mask covered the water. The darkness of night stormed in on the heels of the fleeting sunlight. As I looked up above me, the sky glowed with a mix of orange, red and purple swatches all caught up in a westward race away from the chasing blackness. My gaze dropped to the water. The breaking waves rolled in, crashing against the sand in a melodious rhythm.

I pushed away from the window as the long shadows filled the room. They seemed to engulf me as I backed away and collapsed onto the stool. One shadow began to work its way across the painting, cutting its way over Rebecca's face. As it passed over her eyes, I could have sworn that her eyes closed for a brief second. I leaned in closer and stared at the painting. Her eyes were open, just as I had painted them.

Shaking my head to clear my thoughts, I turned away from the painting and walked toward the door. I left everything as it was to be taken care of later. The tubes of paint still sat out beside the brushes. The full range of the emotional spectrum, from happiness to grief, nervousness to relief, had me under constant bombardment since I first sat down and picked up a brush earlier. I passed through the doorway into the hall and felt a great weight lifted from my shoulders as I escaped my own self-imposed mental prison for the day.

I walked through the dim hallway toward the kitchen to fix something to eat. A sudden, staggering hunger consumed me.

My stomach scolded me for ignoring it all day, but at the same time my heart and mind rebuked it, telling me that I had done exactly what I needed to do.

Mental and emotional exhaustion washed over me, which led to physical exhaustion. The bed looked very inviting as I stepped into the bedroom after eating dinner. Without even changing, I collapsed on the mattress and curled up into a ball, pulling the comforter around me to shield out the world. My mind replayed the events of the day within the theater of my head. Safe and secluded in bed, the emotions began building up once again. So much had happened that I hadn't been able to fully process each event as it occurred. It was all catching up to me, bombarding me. I pulled the comforter over my head and wrapped my arms around the pillow, squeezing my eyes shut as the tears came.

* * *

That night was the most restful night's sleep I'd had in months. I woke up refreshed and looking forward to the new day, something that hadn't happened in far too long. I ate a bowl of cereal, then ventured back into the studio. It seemed so easy now to just walk into the once off-limits room. A halo of soft morning sunlight surrounded the painting. I crossed the room and sat down on the stool. My hand drifted upwards and stroked Rebecca's painted face.

"Morning, beautiful. I missed you," I whispered, the dried surface of the paint smooth and fine to the touch. "I thought about you all night long."

It almost seemed like everything was back to normal, if only for a brief instant. I woke up early in the morning, as had been my usual routine, and made my way back to the studio. A short time later my conversation with Rebecca would begin. That had been my routine for so many years, only it had been on a hiatus for the past few months. But all seemed well with the world now. I lost myself in the moment, allowing it to fully consume me.

"I hope you slept well, too. We can see today about finding the perfect spot for you, somewhere a bit more comfortable than the studio. I was thinking either the living room or perhaps back in the bedroom with me. What do you think?"

I didn't really expect an answer, knowing that I was talking to a painting. It was an outlet for me, a way to let out what had been building up inside of me the past few months. All the loneliness and emptiness that I felt could now be released.

"How about some fresh air? It's getting a bit stuffy in here."

I hopped up from the stool and slid the window open. The sweet morning air filtered into the room. A long inhale filled my nostrils with the arousing aroma of the saltwater air. My eyes closed and I pictured the view in my mind's eye as the soothing sounds of the crashing waves and blowing breeze filled my ears. For the first time in a long time, everything felt right.

Shaking free from the brief daydream, I pulled myself away from the hypnotic setting beyond the window and sat back down in front of the easel. The painting encompassed my entire field of vision, entrancing me as I sat there. I got lost in the detail, almost as if I were looking into a window from the outside. Even though nothing moved at all, everything seemed so real, so lifelike. My gaze drifted up to Rebecca's piercing, blue eyes. They were so easy to get lost in. Only one word could describe them—intoxicating. I stared into the sea of blue and imagined that she was staring back down at me. A twinkle lit up her eye.

Outside the window, a cloud passed over the sun, plunging the room into a sudden darkness. I looked out of the window and waited for the cloud to pass. My focus returned to the painting as the unhindered light filled the room once again. As my eyes adjusted, Rebecca's eyes seemed to track from the window back to me. I shook my head and blinked several times. My eyes had to be playing tricks on me. It had to be a fluke from the passing cloud, I convinced myself. I tried to push the thought out of my mind as I leaned in closer to the painting. My fingertips caressed Rebecca's cheek.

"You have no idea how much I miss you. It kills me inside knowing that I'll never get to hold you again."

My head dropped into my hands and I hunched forward. A wave of sorrow rushed over me. I managed to raise my head and look at Rebecca through my tear-filled eyes. Her blue eyes glistened in the soft light. A single tear escaped her eye and carved a path down her cheek. I jumped up from the stool. My legs almost failed me and I stumbled backward. The table buckled under the sudden weight of my collapse. The cup of water flew off the table. My hand hit the brushes. The palette hit the floor with a crash. Breath came in labored gasps. I almost slipped on the wet spot in the carpet. My only thought was to run out of the room. I never looked back as I stumbled into the hall.

Chapter Eighteen

My steps faltered as I stumbled down the hall. The air seemed thin, almost as if it were being sucked from the house. Every inhalation met with a vicious struggle to breathe. I made it to the front door and yanked it open. A sudden rush of cool air blasted against my face and filled my exhausted lungs. I staggered onto the porch. My legs began to regain their strength as I leaned against the railing and took several slow, deep breaths.

I had to be going crazy. That had to be it. My mind struggled around what happened with the painting. Everything was still a jumble of random, incoherent thoughts and feelings. Paintings don't just start changing on their own, at least not that I'd ever seen.

Squeezing the handrail, I eased down the steps and walked across the grass toward the beach. The haste to escape from the studio and, subsequently, from the house left me barefoot. The ground felt hard and cold beneath my feet, but once I reached the sand, it changed to a soft coolness.

I paced back and forth along the shoreline until I regained

enough composure to attempt to go back inside. My eyes remained fixed on the open front door and my path to the studio. Everything else blurred into the background as if I wore blinders. The next thing I knew I was standing in the hall outside the studio eyeing the interior. The painting rested on the easel in full view of the door. My eyes locked onto Rebecca's before I even entered the room. Her shimmering, blue eyes seemed to gaze back at me. I inched my way into the room shrouded with a heightened anticipation. My gaze never once strayed from the painting. Pausing in front of it, I leaned to each side and eyed the portrait.

Everything seemed normal enough. Maybe it was all in my head. I shuffled back and forth in a lazy semicircle around the easel and scrutinized the painting from every angle. After several passes, there was nothing—no movement, no changes. Rebecca's eyes remained fixed, frozen, staring straight forward.

"This is crazy. Nothing's going to change."

Keeping my eyes on the painting, I found the stool with my hand and sat down. The breath that I had been holding silently escaped. I dropped my head and massaged the back of my neck. The muscles began to relax. The tension escaped through the gentle pressure of my fingertips. My eyes drifted up to look at Rebecca once more. I sprang up from the stool. Instead of being fixed, staring straight forward, Rebecca's eyes were looking down at me. I backed away from the painting. I kept the stool between me and the easel. It served as a weak barrier from the portrait. Rebecca's eyes followed me the entire time as I moved my head around. Her abrupt blink sent me running out of the room again.

I rushed out of the studio and grabbed the phone from the table in the living room. I punched the buttons of the phone, dialing Kelly's number as I fell on the couch. My fingertips pounded the armrest. After an eternity, someone on the other end picked up.

"Hello?" a child's voice asked.

"Sean, it's Uncle Martin. Is your mom there?"

"Hey, Uncle Martin," Sean's voice perked up. "Guess what happened today?"

Obviously, I misjudged the attention span of an eight year old boy, but I indulged his enthusiasm. "What happened?"

"I was playing in the backyard and I found a chipmunk. You know, like Chip and Dale. So anyway, mom said I could keep him if I took care of him. Isn't that great?"

"That's great, Sean," I responded, masking my impatience. "Can you go get your mom for me?"

"Oh, yeah, hold on. I'll go find her." A loud clunk passed through the earpiece and I heard his footsteps scampering away as he called for his mother. A moment later heavier footsteps approached the phone before Kelly picked up the handset.

"Hello?"

"Kelly, it's Martin."

"Oh, hey. I was about to call you in a little since I haven't talked to you in a couple of days. Is everything okay?"

"No, something's happening."

"What?"

"I'm not sure," I answered, pausing to gather my words before continuing. "I don't really know. It's the painting."

"What do you mean 'the painting'?"

"Rebecca's painting. The portrait I was in the middle of doing for her when she got sick."

"I never saw any painting," Kelly replied.

"That's because I closed off the studio the night you sent me home from the hospital to clean up. I hadn't worked on it, gone into the studio, or even picked up a brush in the past four months, at least until yesterday. I finally kept my promise to Rebecca and finished her painting last night."

"I bet that was hard for you. So what did you mean by 'it's the painting'?"

"I don't really understand it yet myself," I explained, unsure of what I was trying to tell her. I wasn't even sure what to believe myself. "But can you come down here?"

Kelly remained quiet for a moment as I waited. "I don't know. Jesse's got the science fair coming up and still has a lot of work to do on his entry that I was supposed to help him with."

"Even for a day or two? Three tops," I pressed. "I can't really explain it, but I might be losing it. There's just so much going on. I don't know if I can handle it."

The line went silent. I could hear nothing, not even the sound of her breathing. A minute later, she responded.

"Um, I could see if Mark's sister can watch the kids again and maybe I could come down tomorrow. Would that work?"

"That'll be fine. Thanks, I mean it."

"It's no problem. I'll see you tomorrow."

"Bye," I replied back, then dropped the handset on the cradle.

I lingered on the couch for a few seconds, just staring at the phone. Pushing myself up, I walked through the hall. Though what was happening made no sense and was freaking me out, I still found myself drawn back to the studio and the painting. I froze outside the door and stared into the room as if I were inspecting an alien environment, not the room where I spent much of the last twenty years. I gave in and walked through the door and into the empty studio.

Although I was the only one in the house, I still closed the door behind me then crossed the room to close the blinds, not wanting to be seen. But who would believe this anyway? I'm still not sure if I even believe it. Then a thought hit me. I froze with my hands on the blinds. What about Kelly? Was I right in calling her about this? A flood of possibilities rushed through my head. What if she told someone else? What if she doesn't believe me? What if she thinks I'm crazy? What if I really am crazy? Stuff like this doesn't happen to normal people.

I squeezed my eyes shut and shook my head in a vain attempt to force out the thoughts. I crossed the room and sank down in front of the easel. My eyes were fixed on the image of Rebecca in the painting as she sat on the couch, staring out of the window at the mid-morning sunrise over the water.

As I leaned forward to get a better look, the changes in the painting became glaringly apparent to me. Rebecca now sat facing the window as opposed to looking straight forward. Another detail was the roses that I added. Instead of being on her lap, two were on the couch next to her and the other two were lying on the floor.

So many things raced through my mind that I wasn't sure what to think or what to believe. How could this be happening? I had heard stories of haunted paintings before, such as a ship moving across the water or a light coming on in the window of a house, but I never believed the stories. It was always explained to be supernatural or paranormal. But now it was happening to me. So what exactly did that mean?

My mind began to spin under the weight of all my debating. I needed fresh air, but I didn't want to leave the room. And I definitely didn't want to leave the painting. I hopped up and pulled up the blinds. A rush of cool, fresh air filtered into the room when I opened the window. Leaning on the windowsill with my face pressed against the screen, the air rushed into my lungs as I remained by the window for a moment just sucking in deep breaths.

A refreshing calmness soaked into my bones. I pushed myself away from the window and collapsed back onto the couch. The easel faced the wrong way for me to be able to see anything. I repositioned it so that the portrait faced the couch, and then I fell back into the seat with my eyes locked on the painting. Nothing else mattered other than sitting here with Rebecca. Thankfully, it was the weekend and I didn't have to worry about being gone for most of the day at work.

"Work!" I exclaimed aloud as I straightened up on the couch. Having to leave the next morning was the last thing I wanted to do, but I couldn't just not show up, especially after everything Paul's done for me lately.

There had never been a phone in my studio because I didn't want the distraction so I ran to the kitchen. I grabbed the phone and dialed the number for Paul's cell phone. He answered after three rings.

"Martin!" he shouted. "How are you?"

I paused for a second, caught off-guard, but then realized that he probably just checked the caller ID as he answered.

"It's going," I answered cryptically. "What about you?"

"Oh, the usual. Busy, busy, busy."

"Listen, the reason I called is that I need a big favor and I didn't know who else to ask."

The other end of the line got quiet for a second. Paul's voice turned serious. "Sure, anything. What is it?"

Before answering, I hesitated for a second to organize my thoughts. "I need to take some personal time off from work. Some things have come up that I need to direct my full attention to."

"What's going on? Is there something wrong? Talk to me."

For a second, I contemplated telling him what was happening, but my cautiousness got the best of me before I answered. "I can't really talk about it right now. In all honesty, I don't even know what's going on. But it's nothing bad, just something personal I have to take care of."

"You sure?" he questioned. I could hear the concern in his voice.

"I'm sure."

"How much time do you need?"

I hadn't thought that far ahead yet. After a few quick calculations, I answered. "Just a few days, maybe a week at most. I'm not entirely sure."

"Well, take whatever time you need. I'll make sure to clear it with the site manager. It won't be a problem."

A sense of relief passed over me. "Thank you, Paul. Thanks a lot."

"No problem. And thank you for calling me."

"Well, I'll let you get back to whatever you were doing."

Paul spoke up. "Oh, if you ever want to talk about whatever is going on, or anything else for that matter, I'm always here. Day or night, you can always call."

"I'll keep that in mind. I'll talk to you later."

"Take care."

I hung up the phone and rushed back into the studio. The breeze blew through the open window. Though it was only late afternoon, darkness already hovered in the distance out over the water. Threatening grey clouds rolled toward the shore along the upper currents, bringing with them a large shadow covering the rippling surface of the water. There would most certainly be a storm sometime tonight.

A yawn forced its way from my mouth before I had the chance to stifle it. I checked the clock again to make sure of the time. Fatigue worked its way through my body even though it was still early. Why I felt that way eluded me since I had a restful night's sleep. Instead of fighting the feeling, I curled up on the couch with my arms clutching one of the pillows. The room plunged into dimness from the passing of one of the clouds over the sun. The entire time, my eyes never left the portrait. I stared at Rebecca through the darkness.

My eyes grew heavy. The cloud still covered the sun, as if it were unable to pass. I strained to focus on Rebecca's face, searching for any type of movement, anything at all, but I could see nothing. The breeze turned from cool to cold as it blew through the window. The air hit my face which sent a chill running down my spine and caused my whole body to shudder. I pulled the afghan down from the back of the couch and wrapped it around me. My gaze shifted over toward the window, knowing that if I closed it, I wouldn't be so cold. But there was something about having it open. I closed my eyes and listened to the sounds drifting in. The light crash of the waves filtered in, only to be interrupted a moment later by the shrill squawking of a crane riding high on the currents.

*   *   *

A jagged bolt of lightning carved its way through the blackness of the night, lighting up the entire sky. Seconds later, a rumbling thunderclap growled and shook the house. My eyes snapped open as I was yanked out of an uneasy sleep. I strained through the darkness to see the clock. It was nearly ten. I didn't remember falling asleep, though I recalled nodding in and out a few times. Another bolt of lightning illuminated the sky, cutting through the long shadows of the room. Rebecca's eyes lit up from the flash.

I draped the afghan around my shoulders and pushed myself up from the couch, crossing the room to the open window. I leaned on the windowsill and closed my eyes as I listened to the pattering of the raindrops outside. The breeze felt cool against my face. There was something familiar in the smell of it, something more than the usual saltwater air. The temperature had dropped noticeably over the past couple of hours since it started raining. I pulled the afghan tighter around my body.

Turning away from the window, my gaze drifted around the room. The couch looked inviting as always. As I curled back up under the afghan, the familiar scent grew stronger than before. It was intoxicating. I took another, slower, deep breath, allowing the scent to fill my lungs. I recognized the fragrance as Rebecca's. The time she spent on the couch watching me paint had embedded her scent into the fabric. I couldn't believe that I was just now noticing it.

My head rested on the pillow as I clutched the afghan tighter. I looked up at the painting. Rebecca's face was once again illuminated by the flashes of lightning outside the window. I settled back onto the couch. Everything began to fade as I drifted in and out of consciousness. The sounds of thunder and flashes of lightning grew quieter until all I heard was the methodic crashing of the waves and the hypnotic drumming of the raindrops outside the window.

For the rest of the night, I drifted in and out of sleep. I

woke up several times and just stared at the painting through the darkness. I finally fell into a restless sleep in the early morning hours as the first rays of the sun peeked over the horizon.

Chapter Nineteen

Hello?" A voice called out from the front of the house. "Anybody home? Martin?"

My eyes snapped open and I remembered that Kelly was supposed to drive down today. I threw the afghan aside and jumped up from the couch.

"Kelly? That you?" I asked as I hurried toward the living room.

"Yeah, it's me. I knocked a couple of times but you didn't answer. So I used the spare key to let myself in."

I found Kelly standing in the foyer with a small overnight bag at her feet. She hung her jacket behind the door and then stared at me, eyebrow raised. "Did I wake you up?"

It was obvious that I had just gotten up. The reflection in the hall mirror said it all. My hair stuck out in a hundred different directions. The clothes I had on were the same I had worn all day yesterday and were completely wrinkled.

"Actually, yeah, you did," I answered, rubbing my eyes with both hands.

"Picking up the habit of sleeping late now, I take it?"

"Sleeping late?"

"Yeah, it's after ten. I left around seven, once I got the kids ready for school. You made it sound like it was important on the phone yesterday, so I figured I'd get here as soon as possible."

"You really didn't have to come so early. I think I might have made it out to sound more important than it actually is."

Kelly stared at me, her eyes unwavering. "Yeah, I don't buy it. What's really going on?"

Again I silently questioned whether calling Kelly had been the right thing to do. Maybe telling her would only present more questions than answers. But if I didn't tell her, that would mean she made the trip for nothing, in which case I would feel horrible. My head dropped for a moment before my eyes rose to meet hers.

"There's something you need to see."

Without saying another word, I turned and walked back toward the studio. Kelly followed me but said nothing. We stepped into the room. The afghan lay in a pile on the floor. I folded it and placed it back on the couch.

Kelly remained by the doorway, just looking around the room. "I never realized it until you mentioned it on the phone, but I didn't come in here the whole time I stayed here." She crossed the room and stopped in front of the easel. Her hand reached toward it, but she caught herself and refrained from touching the canvas. "So is this the painting?"

I moved beside her and looked over her shoulder at Rebecca. "Yeah, that's it."

Kelly took my hand and led me over to the couch. As we sat down, she glanced back at the painting, and then focused her attention on me. "So what's going on?"

"Look at that and tell me what you see," I said, nodding toward the canvas.

A crease in her forehead appeared as Kelly scrunched her eyebrows together before turning to look at the easel again. I leaned back on the couch and stared at her as she stared at Rebecca's image. I wondered what she was seeing, what was going on inside of her head. My eyes closed and I visualized the painting in my mind.

After several minutes of intense staring, Kelly turned toward me. Her eyebrows curved upward as a confused look came over her face. "I'm not really sure what I'm looking for. Got a tip, or suggestion, or anything?"

My eyes snapped open as the questions immediately formed inside my head. She couldn't see anything? Why did I see it? Wait, did I really even see anything? I shook my head, wishing that I could make sense of it all.

"Hey, Martin." Kelly waved her hand in front of my face. "You still with me?"

I shook my head and tried to focus in on her. "Yeah, sorry."

"So what's this all about?"

"I don't know anymore. I'm just really confused."

Kelly just stared at me for a moment. "Was there something that I was supposed to be looking for in the painting?"

"Yeah, I—no," I stammered. "I don't know."

My eyes closed again as I tried to clear my mind. When they opened, I found myself looking up at the painting, Rebecca's face filling my view. I questioned what was happening to me, not knowing what to make of anything anymore. Had I just imagined what I thought I saw?

"I need to eat," I stated without taking my eyes off of the

portrait. "Do you want anything?"

"Yeah, that would be nice."

I continued sitting there for a moment, resisting the urge to get up. Kelly followed my gaze toward the painting and began staring at it herself. The painting seemed to entrance Kelly just as much as it did me.

Pushing all the questions to the back of my mind, I rolled my head from side to side to loosen up my neck. Out of the corner of my eye, a flicker of movement caught my attention. I spun toward the easel and scanned the entire painting in an instant. Instead of her usual expression, Rebecca's eyes were closed and her mouth was open in mid-yawn. I froze where I was on the couch.

Finally able to pry my eyes away, I glanced at Kelly out of the corner of my eye. She sat looking up at the painting, expressionless.

"She had to have seen that," I whispered under my breath. "She had to."

Kelly looked over at me a few seconds later, unfazed. "Did you say something?"

It was right there for her to see. How could she have missed it? The dreadful thought that maybe it really was all in my head flashed through my mind again. Maybe I was going crazy.

I stared back at her. The question she had asked did not register in my mind. Her face still showed no unusual expression, no shock, or surprise. Nothing.

"Hey!" She reached out and shook my arm. "You awake?"

The glaze over my eyes evaporated as I emerged from my daze. Her words exploded through my head. "Huh? Yeah, wait…what?"

Kelly raised her eyebrow at me and just stared. "Are you

okay? You're acting a bit strange, even for you."

I forced my lips to curve upward into an unnatural smile.

"Yeah, I'm fine. Sorry, I just blanked out for a minute. What was I about to do? Oh, food. Did you want anything?"

She nodded then reciprocated my smile. "Yes, please."

Jumping up from the couch, I bounded out of the room, straining to avoid eye contact with the painting. I glanced back over my shoulder as I passed through the door. Kelly got up from the couch and stood inches in front of the painting, still expressionless as she leaned back and forth in front of it.

I hurried into the kitchen and flipped on the lights. My elbows crashed against the counter with the entire weight of my body. My head fell into my hands and plunged my world into sudden darkness. I began questioning my own state of mind and everything that I once thought to be real but pulled myself off of that track, not sure if I really wanted to discover the answer.

After throwing together a quick lunch and setting it out on the table, I called back to Kelly, still in the studio. She joined me in the kitchen and sat down at the table. We ate in an awkward silence for a few moments before Kelly spoke up.

"Are you sure you're okay?"

I placed my sandwich down on the plate as I finished chewing the bite with excruciating slowness. After what seemed like forever, my mouth was finally empty, exhausting my excuses for not responding.

"Yeah, I'm fine. Why?"

"I'm just starting to worry about you. That's all."

I forced a smile along with a muffled chuckle. "Don't worry about it. It's nothing."

Kelly's eyes narrowed into tiny slits as she glared back at

me. "Don't give me that. I've known you long enough to see past your excuses. I mean, first it was the phone call yesterday, then you were acting weird just a few minutes ago. So tell me what's going on or, so help me God, I'll leave."

My eyes rose to meet hers and I dropped my shoulders, defeated. After taking a deep breath, I responded. "In all honesty, I don't really know what's going on. I can't figure it out myself. Believe me. It's been on my mind constantly the past day. Every time I think I'm close, everything suddenly changes. I don't think I've ever been so confused in my whole life."

Kelly shrugged off my response as she took a bite of her sandwich. "I think I'm going to take a walk after lunch. You up for joining me?"

Caught off-guard by the sudden shift in topic, I just sat there speechless for a moment before answering. "Yeah, sure."

* * *

A cool breeze blew in from the water. Kelly and I meandered down the beach. A gust of chilled air swept across my cheeks. I readjusted the zipper of my jacket higher and flipped the collar up to shield my neck. Kelly walked beside me, her hands buried in her pockets. As my eyes scanned around, I saw the jetty just ahead and angled off toward it.

We reached the jetty and paused to look out over the water. The gray sky faded into the metallic water making the horizon almost indistinguishable. Just in front of us, small whitecaps crested and then broke, kicking up a mist of spray as they collapsed.

I slowly made my way out on the jetty. Kelly followed me across the rocks. We stopped just above the shallow inlet of calmer water and sat down on one of the larger boulders. The waves crashed into the rocks all around us. I just stared down at my muted reflection in the pool below me.

"So what's really going on?" Her words seemed to float into my head past all my mental barriers, riding on the sounds of the passing waves.

"What do you want me to say?" I conceded, falling prey to the combination of her question and the calming, hypnotizing ocean.

Kelly's lips curved upward into a smile, lightening the mood. "I don't know. If I did, I wouldn't have asked the question, now would I?"

A breathy laugh escaped from my throat as I shook my head at her. It was the only response I could muster.

"So this was your plan for going for a walk? To get me out of the house into a different environment and ask the same exact questions?"

A grin flooded Kelly's face. "Why? Is it working?"

"Just a little."

I broke off and resorted to staring out over the water as I tried to put my thoughts in order. After a short pause, I recounted the events of the past couple of months since Kelly left, up until a few days ago.

"Things were really starting to get bad."

Kelly nodded in agreement. "I can see that."

"But then I was watching the video of Cheryl's first birthday up here and something Bec said caught my attention. It was almost as if she was talking to me now. That's what provoked me to finish the painting, even after so long."

Not speaking, Kelly just sat there looking back at me. Her gaze broke away and she stared out toward the horizon. A thoughtful, almost confused, expression clouded her face.

"So that's why you called me? Because you finished the

painting?"

"Not exactly," I answered, unsure of what more to say. Everything had been building up inside of me over the past day, bursting to get out, but was it really such a good idea? Kelly had been sitting right there when I saw things move and she hadn't seen, or noticed, anything.

"What exactly does that mean?"

My mouth opened to answer, but no words came out. A warm breath escaped, condensing into a misty cloud in front of my face. I closed my mouth and, out of the corner of my eye, I saw Kelly staring at me with her eyebrows raised.

"I called because I saw things changing in the painting," I blurted out.

With my eyes closed, I turned my head toward Kelly, unsure if I wanted to see her expression. When I opened my eyes, her face was blank.

"I really have no clue what's going on. One minute it's exactly as I painted it, the next it's different. It can't just be all in my head, or at least I thought it couldn't. But then earlier, I watched the painting change while we were in the studio before eating. When I looked at you, you didn't seem to notice anything." I paused for a second to catch my breath before continuing. "I just don't know what to think. I know in my mind that it can't really be happening, but I pray in my heart that it is. I mean, I see things changing in the painting. I know it can't be real, right? It's impossible."

Kelly's response came in a whisper barely louder than the sounds of the surrounding ocean. "I would have probably agreed with you yesterday."

Her eyes scanned the horizon before resting on me. I stared back at her as the words sank in, although still not fully comprehending what she was saying.

"I would have listened and then given a reason for why it was all in your head," she continued, speaking a little louder. "But I can't do that anymore. I can't sit there and tell you reasons why you couldn't have seen something when I have seen things myself."

"What did you just say?" My jaw hung open. "You saw it, too? But I watched you. You showed no signs of seeing anything at all."

"I'm sorry I didn't say anything sooner. I wasn't sure what I saw, or what to believe. All I can say is that I panicked and I froze. And that I'm sorry."

I shook my head as I reached out and put my hand on her shoulder. "You don't have anything to be sorry for."

"When I first saw it, I thought I was going crazy for a minute."

I started laughing. "I know what you mean."

The laughter died out. We said nothing for the longest time, just holding each other's gaze, before Kelly broke off and looked out over the water. Her eyes tracked a pair of seagulls riding the breeze above us.

"What exactly did you see in the painting?" I asked after waiting several minutes.

Kelly looked over at me. Her face mirrored the same uncertainty and confusion that I had felt earlier. I forced myself to relax and my expression to be inviting and calm, all the while nervousness and anticipation crept in, threatening to taking over.

"At first, I saw her blink, but I thought it was just a shadow or something. Then she turned her head and looked out the window."

"All this happened while I was sitting next to you?"

"Yeah."

"I would have never known if you hadn't told me. Your face showed nothing at all."

Kelly paused for a second and took a slow, deep breath. "So is that what you saw?"

"That's what I saw last night. But it was different earlier today when we were in there."

Kelly's eyebrows scrunched together as her head tilted to the side. She started to speak, but nothing came out.

"What I saw earlier today was Rebecca yawning," I continued. "Last night, she was in a completely different pose from the one I painted. She was looking out the window with the roses on the floor, whereas I painted her looking straight forward with the roses in her lap."

"How is it possible for us to see two different things when looking at the same painting at the same time?"

"How is it possible for the painting to change in the first place?"

Kelly pressed her lips into a thin line and shrugged her shoulders. She turned her attention back out over the water. I followed her gaze out to a small fishing trawler pushing through the water. Two seagulls fighting in the water down the shore brought us out of our silence.

"So what happens now?" she asked.

"I have no idea. But at least there's one upside of this that I can see."

"What's that?"

"It's not just me. So unless we are both simultaneously going insane, I'm not crazy."

"Yeah, I can see how that would be a plus." Kelly paused to

look down at her reflection in the pool below us then back at me. "So what do we do next?"

"We?" I echoed. "So it's going to be the both of us?"

"Yeah, unless that's a problem. I mean I'm as much a part of this now since I've seen things change, too, unless mental illness is contagious and you've somehow infected me. In which case, I'll be a tad bit bitter."

Her smile brightened up the gray, overcast sky. As I looked over at Kelly, I found myself smiling back at her.

"Have you thought about doing another painting to see if anything else happens? That's the one thing I've learned from helping Jesse do his science fair project. When you have something happen, you repeat the process to see if it happens again."

"Actually, no, the thought hadn't crossed my mind. But I have been preoccupied with things, as you can see."

"Obviously," Kelly stated.

"But it is a good idea. The only question now is what to paint."

"I'm sure you'll figure something out. I have faith in you."

Chapter Twenty

I sat alone on the couch in the studio as Kelly scavenged through the kitchen for something to eat. The question still weighed heavily on my mind: what should I paint? I kept drawing a blank. The easel faced the couch so that Rebecca's face stared down at me. Every so often I would look up at her, wishing I could ask her for advice. If only she could tell me how she wanted to be painted.

My head fell back onto the couch and I stared up at the ceiling for a moment before closing my eyes. My mind wandered through old memories and conversations. Something kept pulling at me. No matter where my thoughts veered off to, they always ended up back at the porch swing, overlooking the ocean. I knew that wasn't what I should paint. It would be no different than the couch scene, just a different location. There had to be something more to it.

I cycled through my memories, starting at the end. The last time Rebecca was on the swing was the morning we sat out for a while before breakfast, a few weeks before she died. But why was that so important? Why that particular time? She must have said something that was relevant to painting. But what was it?

The scene played in my mind starting with the conversation about the nervousness of the upcoming radiation therapy. After that, Kelly came out to tell us that breakfast was ready, but we didn't go inside just then. No. We stayed on the swing and she started talking about birds. About soaring without a care in the world. But what specifically did she say? I squeezed my eyes tighter trying to recall her words.

I've dreamt that I was a bird before. Did I ever tell you that?

No, you didn't tell me.

I would be soaring through the clouds, looking down on the world below. I wanted to stay up there forever, but somehow I always ended up back on the ground.

Why's that?

It never failed. I would be flying over the house. When I saw it, I would dive down and fly past. You were always sitting on the porch, looking out over the water. After that, I wanted nothing more than to be back at home with you.

My eyes snapped open. That was what kept pulling me back to the swing. Rebecca dreamt she was a bird flying high above everything. That's how I would paint it, just like her dream.

I shot up off of the couch and spun the easel around as I looked in the corner for a blank canvas. Finding one, my attention focused back on the easel. I didn't want to move Rebecca's portrait, but there was no other free spot. Besides, I wanted Rebecca to be able to see the new painting I was doing for her. A small easel lay half-buried under a few rolls of canvas in the corner. I grabbed it and set the easel up next to the stool and transferred Rebecca's portrait to it so she could watch me work just like she used to do.

I sat in front of the blank canvas with brush in hand. I glanced over my shoulder at Rebecca, watching as she had always loved doing. A light blue layer of paint soon covered most of the canvas. As I painted in the shoreline far below and the tiny details of the house, I realized that this piece was very different from any other painting that I had done in terms of abstractness. Usually everything I painted was realistic and was at least somewhat based off of a real object or person, but the way this one was shaping up broke that mold. I brushed in Rebecca's figure, flying high above the world. The house and the shoreline curved sharply to form a small planet-like ball below her.

With the painting finished, I cleaned the brushes and sat back on the stool in front of the easel. I glanced over at Rebecca, but her eyes were looking straight ahead, oblivious to the new painting. My attention drifted back to the new piece and scanned for any discernable changes. Everything remained just as I painted it a few minutes earlier. Confused and a little disheartened, I rose from the stool and walked toward the kitchen.

Kelly sat at the table, nose buried in the paper, when I walked into the room. She looked up at me when I stopped in the doorway. "How's everything going in there?"

"I finished the painting. But I haven't seen anything yet. Maybe this isn't such a good idea. I mean, it can't be real, right?"

Kelly shrugged. "I don't know. Maybe it takes a little time."

"Or maybe we are both losing our minds. Did you ever stop to think of that?"

"Yeah, actually I did, but it wasn't a solution that I was prepared to accept. Oh, did you get the plate I left in there for you?"

My head tilted to the side as I stared down at her. "You came in while I was painting?"

"Yeah, I fixed lunch and brought it back to you, but you were so engrossed in your work that you didn't even notice. So I just left it on the table beside you."

I backed out of the doorway and headed back to the studio. Kelly hopped up from the table and followed me. As I entered the room with Kelly right on my heels, the plate of food sat on the table, just as she said.

"I must have really been in a zone, or something, not to notice you come in."

Kelly looked up at me, feigning sadness. "I'm shocked that you didn't believe me when I said I brought you lunch. I figured that after all of these years, you wouldn't have doubted me."

Spinning toward her, my hands instinctively shot up into a defensive position. "No, that's not it at all—"

She silenced my reaction with the broad grin spreading across her face. "You'll just never learn, will you?" She reached over and slapped my arm.

"You think you're funny, don't you?"

Kelly nodded.

"Well, I hate to be the one to tell you this. But you're not."

With her lips pressed together, Kelly shook her head and glared at me. She pushed her way past me and sat down on the stool in front of the easel.

"So what's going on with this thing?"

A quiet laugh escaped as I walked up behind her. "I have no idea."

Kelly stared at the painting for a few minutes, occasionally leaning in to look closer at a particular area. I stood behind her, watching. My eyes drifted between the two paintings.

"This is so much different from anything else you've ever done. At least anything else that I've seen."

"Good observation. It is somewhat of a departure from my usual paintings. I never really worked on anything surreal before."

"Yeah, I was noticing that. But I have to say, for your first attempt, it's pretty good."

I smiled at her as she looked back to the painting. I reached out for her shoulder and squeezed it. My attention focused on Rebecca in the original portrait. Our eyes seemed to lock together, pulling me in while drowning out the rest of the world. All that existed was her face, particularly her piercing blue eyes fixated back on me.

"I've been thinking…" Kelly's voice pulled me out of my daze.

With a quick shake of my head in an attempt to clear it, I looked over at her.

"We both saw different things at the same time in the same painting, right?" she continued. "So what if it's not the painting but really what we want to see?"

"But what you saw is almost exactly what I saw the first time."

Kelly spun around on the stool for a moment, her lips pressed in a tight line. "Just hear me out. We're both really connected to this painting, you even more so than me. Maybe what we saw was just a manifestation of what we hoped for. We both want a piece of Rebecca to hold on to and to have back with us. Maybe this was just a way for us to get that."

"So you're saying that this second painting isn't going to do anything because it's all in our minds? So then why did I paint it in the first place?"

Kelly stopped spinning in the stool and raised her hands defensively. "Hey, it was just a theory. I never said it was right."

I sat down on the couch and stared at the wall. Of course her theory wasn't right. It couldn't be right. There was no question in my mind that what I saw actually happened. At first I had doubted it, but once Kelly showed up and saw it too, I was convinced. But what Kelly had said a minute ago did make sense from a certain point of view, though I didn't accept that. I needed it to be real.

It occurred to me to try something that I hadn't done, or even wanted to do, in the months since Rebecca had died. I decided to pray. I just wasn't sure where to start or what to say. Everything in my head was a jumble of thoughts. Over the past few months I hadn't wanted anything to do with church or God.

Somehow I managed to put together a coherent prayer, just letting the words and thoughts flow freely within my mind. My prayer was that the connection with Rebecca through the painting be real. Toward the end of my prayer, I heard a faint voice drifting in between the pauses of my unspoken plea. Not sure whether the words were directed at me, or not, I continued with my silent prayer until the speaking grew even louder.

"Um, ignore what I said a minute ago," Kelly's voice echoed through the room.

Pulled back into consciousness, I shook my head before responding. "What did you say?"

"I was wrong earlier when I said that it could be happening just because we wanted it to happen so badly."

My eyebrows straightened into a single line above my eyes as I stared at her, waiting for her to continue her explanation.

"Either I'm really losing it, or it's really happening, because I just saw something. What it was, I'm not entirely sure, but it was something."

A flutter of excitement rose from the depths of my heart. I froze in amazement as I realized that no sooner had I said my prayer than it had miraculously been answered. "What did you see?" I asked, my voiced filled with anticipation.

"The flock of birds that you painted behind Rebecca isn't following her anymore. They went off on their own."

I shot up from the couch and rushed to the easel. Kelly slid off of the stool to allow me to sit down. She leaned on the table and looked over my shoulder at the painting. My eyes flew over the piece and, sure enough, I noticed a few minor changes. A broad smile, echoing my relief, spread across my face.

I settled back on the stool, content in just sitting there and watching. Nothing else mattered. My prayers had been answered almost immediately. It kind of caught me off-guard for a moment, but I resumed gazing at the painting.

*   *   *

Kelly and I eventually pried ourselves away from the studio a few hours later. We sat in the living room after finishing dinner, not saying a word. I spent the time staring at the wall just left of the window. The sun had almost disappeared behind the horizon, ushering in the coming darkness of the sky outside. Fleeting rays of the escaping sunlight peeked in through the window.

Fatigue began to overwhelm me and my eyes closed. I lacked the will to fight the feeling as the darkness overtook me and the vivid dreams began. A deep black filled my view, but I seemed to be moving through it, wandering into the unknown and unseen. A faint glow shone dimly in the distance, growing brighter as I approached. It was only then that I was able to see what was lit. It was the painting of Rebecca sitting on the easel under a bright spotlight in the middle of complete darkness. I stopped in front of the painting, just outside the captivating circle of light.

Rebecca's face stared back at me, her eyes piercing through the lack of light. They called out to me, beckoning me to step forward into the circle. I felt unable to enter into the light, as if it was an impassible barrier, but her blue eyes kept calling to me. Rebecca's face still continued to draw nearer, slow and steady, but I knew that I hadn't moved from my spot just outside the light. I realized that she was breaking free of the painting, pushing out toward me as she tried to escape her current prison of the canvas. My heart began pounding, trying its best to escape from the prison of my own chest. Rebecca's face hovered through the circle of light, drawing nearer to my own. She stopped right in front of me, separated only by the edge of the circle of light. Suddenly everything began to spin out of control.

My eyes snapped open as my chin dropped onto my chest. Even in the dark room the light seemed insanely bright. I squinted until my eyes adjusted. Kelly sat in the chair, no longer in a daze but now looking over at me. My eyes rose to meet her questioning stare.

"What?" I asked, staring back at her, puzzled.

"You okay? You were over there having convulsions."

"Very funny. You know good and well that I just nodded off."

She stared back at me before she smiled. A moment later we were both laughing incessantly, though not knowing just what we were laughing at.

"So I've been thinking," Kelly said. "There has to be some reason that caused the changes in the painting to happen in the first place. I mean, things like this don't just happen on their own without some supernatural help, you know?"

"You have a point."

"Yeah, shocking, isn't it? Every once in a while I do have some good ideas. But really, can you think of anything, anything at all, that is out of the ordinary and could have caused this?"

"Well, there is one thing. I don't know how relevant it is, but it's all I can think of right now." I told Kelly about the night I found Rebecca sitting in front of the half-finished painting, crying. When I finished, Kelly remained quiet for a moment, processing the story. I waited for her to say something, but nothing ever came. "Okay?" I leaned forward toward Kelly. "What's going on in there?"

Her eyes shifted from side to side before looking up at me. She shook her head. "Sorry. I kind of got lost there for a second. Okay, so the only thing you can think of is the night in front of the painting where her tears fell in the paint?" I dropped my chin with a slight nod. "That seems like a good enough reason to me," she continued.

"It's funny. I used to think that all the stories I heard about a painting being haunted, or someone claiming to see something in a picture change from one viewing to the next, were nothing but fantasies in the minds of crackpots. I guess there was some truth to all those other stories; either that, or I have become part of the crackpot group."

"Well, if it's any consolation, I don't think you fall in the category of a crackpot."

I smiled at Kelly, and then my smile turned into a grin. "Thanks, but since you are seeing this as well, you would fall into the crackpot category. So it's not much help for one crackpot to tell another that he isn't one."

"You've got some nerve," Kelly fired back, glaring at me. "How about we just get back to working on the situation at hand?"

"No argument from me there."

So much time and energy and love had been put into the two paintings. They brought me closer to Rebecca than I had felt in all of the months since she was taken from me. There was no way that I was going to let that slip away now. An answer was out there, it had to be. All I had to do was find it. The only question was where to start looking.

Chapter Twenty-One

Kelly left a couple days ago, which was fine with me since we had apparently solved the mystery of the paintings. Well at least what had caused it to happen, at least. Now I had uninterrupted time where I could sit in the studio and paint. If she hadn't left, I doubt that I would have finished seven paintings in two days. The hours seemed to run together. After several more days of straight painting, I had thirteen different paintings of various scenes scattered around the studio. My body and mind were exhausted. I had never painted at such a furious pace in my entire life.

There was just enough space on the couch between two of the paintings for me to collapse on it. My head fell back as I stared straight up at the ceiling. With fatigue setting in, I tried to relax and close my eyes. Something kept nagging at me, telling me that I still was not finished, but I couldn't concentrate or listen to the inner voice in the crowded studio.

I pushed myself up from the couch and shuffled through the house. The bright afternoon sunlight blinded me as I stepped onto the porch. I waited for my eyes to adjust. The warm rays from the sun high above the house beat down on the water, reflecting off the lapping waves back into my face. Moments later, my feet guided me toward my quiet place of solitude. The jetty.

The rocks were a little more slippery than usual as I crossed the boulders. I nearly lost my footing twice but managed to catch myself before falling headlong into the water. I reached my usual spot at the end and sat down on the rocks, feet dangling above the pool. Each crash of the waves against the rocks sent a spray of salty mist into my face, which was both relaxing and soothing.

As calming and serene as this place was, I thought I would be able to figure out the missing piece, the thing that had been nagging at the back of my mind. Instead, I became more frustrated because I could not find the solution. The calming effect faded away. The usual sounds I found so peaceful, like the bird calls and the waves crashing, only seemed to annoy me. I jumped up and rushed back across the jetty toward the beach.

As soon as my feet touched the sand, I froze. The answer hit me as I stood there looking back up the beach toward the house. The picture formed in front of me, almost as if I were standing outside my own body looking down on the scene. A single set of footprints through the sand led from the jetty back to the house. Beside the lone tracks the waves rolled in. The single figure stood on the sand looking back along the path of footprints. Everything would lead back to the focal point of the painting: our home.

My incompetence slapped me square in the face. The answer had been right under my nose the whole time, yet I had failed to see it. I hurried back toward the house and frantically cleared out space in the studio to start a new painting. My mind was a flurry of excitement and anticipation. As I picked up a couple tubes of paint, I realized they were almost empty, but I had just enough left to do the painting, if used sparingly.

There was a strange feeling in the air around me as I picked up a brush and squeezed some paint onto the palette. As I mixed the Titan Buff with the smallest dab of black, the realization of the feeling hit me. All the previous paintings I had done of Rebecca led up to this one. It was the last one in the series.

That got me thinking. If Rebecca's crying into the paints really was the answer to the mystery, what would happen when the last of that paint had been used up? What would I do then? That scenario was unacceptable to me. I had to do something, anything, to keep my connection with her from fading away.

The smell of the paints soon filled the room, the aroma as sweet as the ocean air. The brush in my hand felt as if it were an extension of my own body.

The studio was more crowded than I would have liked, but I didn't want to move any of the paintings. It sounded strange, but I liked having all of the Rebeccas surrounding me, watching me paint a new piece of her. There was comfort in spending all day in the studio now, able to spend as much time as I wanted with Rebecca that I had been so wrongfully denied earlier.

My thoughts drifted back to the canvas in front of me. Much to my surprise, I had painted the beach and the water while lost in thought. I set the palette and brush down on the table and gazed into the painting, appearing so vivid, so real. It was soothing and calming, yet at the same time out of place. Something was missing. I wandered around the scene in my mind's eye, searching. The sand looked perfect in front of me, only missing the trail of footprints at the moment. The breaking waves curled over the sand. My eyes drifted upward to the blue sky. Billowing white clouds hung frozen in space, but something was still missing. There were no clouds, no birds, nothing.

I grabbed another brush and mixed together a light gray beside a dab of white. The fine bristles soaked up the monotone gray. The short strokes moved across the canvas, filling in the bodies of a flock of seven birds flying in formation over the water. I dipped the brush into the white and added the highlights to their bodies.

I looked over at the portrait of Rebecca sitting beside me. "It's beautiful, isn't it? The piece is starting to shape up. It won't be long now."

The brush continued to stroke across the canvas as if it had a mind of its own. My hand obediently followed along. The trail of footprints appeared in the sand. Higher on the beach, clumps of grass grew on the sides of the dunes. They curved under the soft breeze blowing in from the water.

"Looks just like it, doesn't it?" I asked, glancing over at Rebecca but not missing a stroke. "Soon you'll be back home where you belong."

I realized that once again I went all day without eating. If Kelly had still been here, she would have scolded me over and over again, forcing me to eat. Something deep inside me knew that she was right and was just looking out for me, even though I always fought her on the subject. Giving into the battle to break from painting, I rose to my feet and forced myself to head toward the kitchen.

It was a short break, ten minutes at most, but a break nonetheless. I ate a peanut butter and jelly sandwich and some chips. After running water over the dishes and leaving them in the sink, I took a moment to walk out onto the porch. My eyes fell shut as I leaned against the railing. The sounds were exactly the same as from inside the studio. With a sudden urge, I rushed back into the house and grabbed the phone, then proceeded to punch the buttons. The line began to ring and a few seconds later Kelly answered on the other end out of breath.

"Hello?"

"Hey, it's Martin."

"Hey! Sorry it took so long to answer. I was outside with the kids." She paused. "Is everything going okay? It's good to see that you finally took a break from painting. I was beginning to wonder if you even noticed I left since I hadn't heard from you."

"Ha ha, you're funny. Everything is fine. But I got to thinking about things after you left." I tried to think of the best way to word my question. "Did you tell Mark anything?"

Kelly remained silent for a moment before answering. "No, I didn't. He asked about it when I got home the other day, but I wasn't sure exactly what to tell him so I just shrugged it off. He hasn't really asked anything since."

"Oh, I'm sorry about that."

"What for? You didn't do anything."

"Yeah, I know, but if it wasn't for me and this whole thing, you wouldn't have had to try to figure out what to tell him and what not to tell."

"Hey, don't talk like that." The sternness in her voice traveled through the line as clear as if she were standing right in front of me. "None of this is your fault and I'm just as much a part of it now as you are. So don't go saying things like that."

I couldn't help but smile. "Yes, mother."

"Okay, now that's much better," she replied. "So what's going on?"

"Oh, I just wanted to fill you in on the last few days with the painting."

As soon as I caught her up, I was off of the phone and walking back to the studio. My steps echoed through the quiet hall. The first thing I did after walking into the room was cross over to the window and pull back the blinds. The room filled with an orange-ish glow, all that remained of the day. I paused to stare out of the window as the dark clouds of the coming night rolled in over the water. It took some effort, but I pulled myself away from the view out the window. I flipped the light switch on. The faint light from the window turned into a bright whiteness as the overhead bulb began to glow.

I sat back down at the easel and grabbed the brush. My eyes drifted over the canvas, following the brush strokes in the dried paint. The picture in my mind flashed back to the view from the sand in front of the jetty earlier in the day. It was frozen in my mind, a picture of perfection. I looked back at the canvas. The painting was half-finished. The sand, beach and sky were complete. All that remained was to paint the house, the jetty, and Rebecca.

The brush slid across the taut canvas with ease, leaving a thin trail of paint in its wake. I dipped the brush back into the brownish mixture and swept the bristles in short strokes, cutting the vague shape of the house into the background. After mixing in some black to darken the tone of the color, I stroked in the shadows and lowlights of the clapboard siding. The next task was to add the windows, and then came the porch and yard. I filled the palette with a variety of bright colors, from yellow to blue to purple. A few swipes of the brush and the yard exploded with color. Every flower was in full bloom, brilliant and beautiful, just the way Rebecca and I had planned. She had always loved working in the yard when she wasn't at the shop. I added the grass and cut the faint path from the house to the beach, passing between the two sand dunes.

I felt like I was standing in the painting, looking around. Everything was bright and clear. A smile came to my face as I traced the brush strokes along the freshly painted clapboard siding of the house. My gaze wandered around the inside of the painting, down the trail from the house to the beach, then along the path of footprints. There was only one thing left to paint. Then, and only then, the painting would be complete.

A loud thunderclap exploded outside the window, shaking the entire house. It was enough to snap me out of my daydream and back to reality. I crossed the room to the open window and peered out into the darkness. The sky filled with streaks of lightning out toward the darkening horizon. A few seconds later, another explosion thundered through the air.

I backed away from the window, leaving it open. The sound of the first few drops hitting the ground filled the room. Sitting back down at the easel, my eyes scanned over the painting. The only thing left to paint was Rebecca.

With brush in hand, I began to paint in her figure. She stood on the beach next to the jetty, looking up the trail of footprints to the house. Her light blue sundress was frozen in place, caught mid-wave in the breeze. She stood barefoot in the sand. The sun shone high above her and cast a short shadow beside her.

The painting was now finished. I sat back and just stared at it. There was only one word to describe it: incomplete.

Something was still missing from it. I looked around the painting, searching for anything that seemed out of place but found nothing. My eyes searched the piece time after time. Nothing seemed to be missing.

I decided to experiment. With my eyes closed and brush in hand, I let my hand roam around the canvas. It came to rest in a spot just above the fabric. I opened my eyes. The tips of the bristles were hovering just beside Rebecca. Then it occurred to me. This was the last painting, so why did Rebecca have to be alone? There was nothing left for me here, nothing stopping me from doing whatever I needed to do to join her.

The decision calmed me and settled my nerves in an instant. I knew what I needed to do as I glanced away from the canvas at myself, at what I was wearing. It was good enough. I dipped the bristles into the paint and added a figure standing next to Rebecca, wearing the same cutoff pants and button-down shirt that I had on. I painted my hand intertwined in hers as we stood on the beach together.

I set the brush and palette on the table and eased back on the stool. My eyes remained fixed on the two of us standing beside the jetty, hand in hand. Now everything was as it should be, as it was always meant to be. I sat there just staring at the canvas, basking in the calmness that filled my thoughts and relaxed my body. Now the painting was complete.

I sat in front of the painting long into the early morning hours, just staring at Rebecca and me alone on the beach. Our beach. There was nothing that could ever tear us apart again. We would now be together forever. That was unchangeable. My emotions began taking over my body. The tears formed in my eyes. I grabbed a pen and a sheet of paper from the table and scribbled down the thoughts collecting inside my head. I walked out to the living room and sat down at the desk in the corner. My hand shook as I retrieved an envelope from the drawer and addressed it. I folded the paper and slid it inside, then sealed the envelope.

The air outside hit my face and sent a slight chill through my body. The air smelled fresh, the just after a storm scent. Another front was coming in across the water. It would be here any day now. But none of that mattered now. I walked to the mailbox and put the letter inside, pulling up the red flag on the side. As I turned away, I stopped. The ocean was magnificent. The sun teasingly peeked over the horizon. I had never seen it look as beautiful as it did at this very moment. It was exactly how I wanted to remember it. A sudden rejuvenation flowed over my body as I walked down the path between the two sand dunes toward the water.

Epilogue

Kelly closed the worn leather journal, feeling the rough texture under her fingertips, and stood up from the couch. She arrived earlier that morning after receiving Martin's letter in the mail. The entire trip back was a blur. Her mind was in shambles, not knowing what the letter meant or what she would find once she got to the house.

The rain beat down on the roof, pounding the shingles with each drop. Gray clouds stretched across the horizon as far as the eye could see. Whitecaps broke against the shoreline just past the dunes where the wind whipped through the long grass. She watched as the drops of rain splattered and disappeared into the churning ocean. Even with the storm raging outside, it seemed quiet, as if the inside of the house was a vacuum. It felt quite unnerving to actually be in the middle of it all, the turmoil outside combined with the unsettling silence inside.

The only light in the house came from the windows. Kelly had opened the blinds once she arrived. Everything in the air— the smell and feel of the house, the storm—pointed to one sensation…gloomy. She fell back on the couch. A thin layer of dust covered the coffee table. She traced her finger through the dust, leaving a faint but visible line. Her eyes drifted around the room. Every piece of furniture was also covered by dust. She took a deep breath, which led to a violent coughing spat. She walked into the kitchen and got a glass from the cupboard. There were pitifully few options to choose from in the refrigerator, a half-empty gallon of milk, a carton of orange juice and a swig of coke in a two-liter bottle.

Kelly grabbed the milk and closed the refrigerator door. She set the glass down on the counter and removed the cap. A sudden putrid smell overwhelmed her senses. She stifled the gag as she poured the milk into the sink. It hit the bottom of the sink and disappeared down the drain, leaving behind a few small clumps. The running water cleared the clumps from the sink, but the rancid smell still remained. She tossed the empty jug into the trash and scolded herself for not checking the expiration date. Assuming the orange juice had likewise gone bad, she poured it down the drain and dropped the carton into the trash as well. Sticking to what was safe she filled the glass with tap water and returned to the living room.

As she sat back down on the couch, she removed the letter from her purse that she received from Martin a day earlier. At first she wasn't going to come. She tried calling him the night before after she read the letter, but there was no answer. So she decided to come up first thing this morning, but not after first spending the entire night reading and re-reading his letter. Her eyes scanned over the paper as she took in the words for what was at least the twentieth time.

Kelly,

Change happens, usually when you least expect it, as we have found out over the past few weeks. Life-changing events come along and you either adjust your course or get left behind. Throughout my entire life, I have never had to make very many difficult decisions. Sure, there were the occasional money issues, a few dry spells here and there, but nothing major. Nothing, that is, until I lost the single most important person in my life. How do you go on after that? When your entire world is thrown upside-down and shaken around, what do you do? You can attempt to go on as normal; but if you have ever actually tried that approach, you'd know it doesn't exactly work. On the other hand, you can try a complete shift with new people, places and activities; but that generally doesn't work, either. So what, you might ask, is the sure-fire, easy solution to deal with change? Honestly, I have no idea. But if I find out, I'll make sure to let you know.

Five months ago, I lost my wife, my soul mate, the person I spent the past thirty-two years of my life with. At the same time, you lost your sister and best friend. So you are the person who can best relate to what I have been going through. Everything you have done has meant so much to me, especially the time you left your own family to come stay with me. I could have never in my life shown you how much that meant to me. You will always have my thanks and admiration for that.

But now a new situation has presented itself before me. By some improbable opportunity, it seems that I have the slightest chance of getting my life back, of getting Rebecca back. No matter how much of a long shot it might be or how risky it may seem, it is something that I must do, not just for me but for Rebecca as well. I hope that you understand where I'm coming from and why I have to do this. I don't know when we will see each other again, but we will always have our connection to the paintings. Feel free to take any of the paintings from the studio that you want. But please take the last piece that I did, the one of Rebecca and me together. I want you to take that one home with you. It would mean a great deal to me. I also left you a leather journal on the coffee table.

Please take that and read it at some point. Hopefully, it will explain everything.

Thank you for all that you've done for me. I will never forget it.

All my love,

Martin

Her hand shook uncontrollably as she folded the letter and returned it to the envelope. The leather journal sat on the table beside her purse. The storm outside seemed to have simmered down. The once pounding rain now pattered melodically against the roof. It was almost calming. She closed her eyes and allowed the gentle sounds to wash over her body. Over the melody of the falling rain, she heard the soft crashing of the waves. She couldn't remember how long she sat on the couch, just listening to the rain, but when she broke out of the trance, she was calm and relaxed. She pushed herself to her feet.

Just like the living room, the studio was covered with a thin layer of dust. A dozen or so paintings were scattered about the room, either on the couch, easels, or leaning up against the wall. The curtains were closed so the room was shrouded in darkness. All her calmness vanished as she felt claustrophobic in the dark, cluttered room. She backed away from the door and hurried out to the porch. The rain splattered around her as she leaned against the railing and stared out over the water.

She needed to catch her breath. The ocean always seemed to be able to clear her head. She guessed she was more like Martin than she realized. She frowned at neglecting to bring a change of clothes so she could take a quick run down the beach. Running right after it had rained always invigorated her and was one of her favorite things to do.

With a revived focus, she pushed away from the railing and walked back inside. She opened each window along the way back to the studio. A fresh breeze blew in, filling the house with the crisp ocean air.

The air filled with dust as she pulled open the curtains in the studio. Holding back a sneeze, she opened the window and took a deep breath of the fresh air as she gazed around the room. It would be hard for her to pick out a couple of paintings to take with her. How could she even begin to choose between them all? They were all so beautiful, and each one was totally different, but they all still had the one common thread, the one meaning: Rebecca.

Her eyes filled with tears as she moved around the room, stopping to glance at each piece. She grabbed the original portrait of Rebecca and leaned it against the doorframe. That was definitely one that she wanted to take. Kelly's eyes lit up as she spied the piece where Rebecca was soaring through the sky, flying above the beach and the house. She set it by the door next to the first one. They were the two that she felt the closest connection to. Her gaze moved over the other paintings. She really wanted to take them all, but resisted the urge and held herself to the two by the door.

A leather portfolio leaned against the wall in the corner. She crossed the room and put the two paintings in the case and set it back down by the door. She walked toward the easel and found herself sitting on the stool, captivated with the last painting. The one Martin wanted her to take as well.

A shiver shot down her spine. The hair on the back of her neck stood on end. This was the first time she had seen the painting that he made such a big deal about. The painting was breathtaking. She found it hard to draw in a breath as her eyes drifted over the canvas. Everything about it pulled her in. It was almost as if she were looking at a photograph taken just down the beach from the house.

Her eyes drifted back and forth from the house, then down the beach, and then to the figures of Martin and Rebecca standing hand in hand beside the jetty. Only one thought dominated her mind: the painting seemed perfect. It looked more complete than any of the previous pieces. It looked happy, fulfilled.

"You did a good job with this one," she whispered. "I hope that you finally found what you were looking for."

A single tear escaped from the corner of her eye and ran down her cheek. She raised her hand to brush it away. Her fingers paused on her cheek for a brief second, and then drifted down to her mouth as she pressed her lips together. She kissed the tips of her fingers and reached out for the canvas. Everything seemed to move in slow motion. It took forever for her hand to reach the painting. But when it did, her hand moved straight toward Martin and Rebecca. She dragged her fingertips down the canvas along their bodies. Her hand dropped to her side as she continued to stare into the painting at the two of them standing together on the sand.

An overwhelming feeling poured over Kelly's body as the tears began to stream down her face. Her hands started shaking again, spreading up her limbs until her whole body began to tremble.

"What am I going to do without you?"

One second she was ecstatic, then heartbroken the next. All the while there was one sentiment that always remained: jealousy. At this moment, Martin had the one thing that she would have given anything to have. He was back with his wife, back with Rebecca. Kelly hated herself for feeling that way. She hated the thoughts that were filling her mind. It took all her strength, all her being, to push them out.

She jumped up from the stool and grabbed the painting from the easel. Another portfolio leaned against the wall beside her. She picked it up and put the last painting inside. One last glance around the room was all her emotions could handle. With the tears streaming, she rushed out of the room, grabbing both portfolios on her way out.

*   *   *

A cool breeze blows across my face. My eyes flutter open, allowing in the light of the mid-afternoon sun shining brightly overhead. Everything is blurry, unfocused. All I hear is the gentle lapping of the waves down by the shoreline. Soon everything begins to grow clearer. The ceiling above the porch swing fills my view. Blinking a few times, my eyes focus. There are faint lines running along the length of each board in the ceiling. As I squint and look closer, the lines seem to fade away right in front of me. I shake my head and look again, but everything appears to be normal. The lines are gone.

I push myself up to a sitting position and gaze out over the beach. The sand is gleaming and completely smooth. The calm water shimmers as it reflects the sun high above. As far as the eye can see, there is nothing but clear blue sky and calm water. I close my eyes and take a slow deep breath. The sweet smell of the salty air fills my nostrils. The scent invigorates my body, flooding my limbs with life. I pull myself to my feet and make my way across the porch and down the steps.

Halfway down the steps, I pause and stare in awe at what is in front of me. The ocean in all its beauty and majesty seemed to be rolling up to my feet. I walk across the sand, feeling my feet sink as the grains conform around my foot and slide between my toes. My eyes close and I stand frozen in the middle of the empty beach with my arms straight out from my shoulders. The cool breeze blows across my face, catching in the folds of my clothes as the fabric trails behind me.

I feel the warmth of the sun beating down on my face, but all I see is the darkness behind my closed eyes. Every sense is heightened. My skin tingles as the air blows over me. As with the other senses, every sound is amplified as well. The wind rips through my hair, sending a low-pitched rumbling through my ears. I hear the crash of the rolling waves in front of me. Overhead, two seagulls squawk obnoxiously as they fly by. Everything seems almost perfect. It suddenly occurs to me that there is only one thing missing, one thing keeping this from being perfect.

My eyes open. It takes a second to readjust to the brightness. A glimmer of movement catches my eye, moving closer to me. I turn in the direction of the shadow and freeze. Rebecca.

As she walks across the sand toward me, I remain frozen in place. My gaze never strays from Rebecca's face as she draws nearer to me. Her arm slips around my own as she stops beside me and just looks out over the water. I look down at her, not knowing what to think. My mouth opens, but no sound escapes. Her gaze drifts from the water up to my face and she smiles at me before resting her head on my shoulder. She wraps her other arm around mine and squeezes it.

The whole time, my eyes never leave her, even as she stands right beside me. I step in front of her, interrupting her view of the ocean. Rebecca's soft blue eyes rise to meet my own. We stand there for the longest moment just gazing at each other. I break the stillness as I ease forward and lower my head toward her. Our lips press together. Even after all this time, I have not forgotten the feel of her lips against mine or the intoxicating smell of her hair or even her taste. Everything is exactly as I remember it being.

With my arms wrapped around her, our lips part. Our faces pause inches apart as we hold each other with a hypnotizing stare. Then, as if drawn by an outside force, I lean in to kiss her once again.

"You have no idea how much I've missed you the past few months."

Her smile seems to light up the entire beach, reflecting the warmth and radiance of the bright sun overhead.

"I knew that you would eventually find a way to come back to me," Rebecca replies. "It was only a matter of time."

We meander our way down the beach, arms interlocked. I pull her close to my body and hold on with everything inside me, never wanting to let her go again.

A Note from the Author

Writing this book has been an interesting and fulfilling challenge. It's an experience I wouldn't change for anything, even if it did take almost two years. I'd like to take a moment to thank all the people who helped me get this book to where it is now.

My parents for all their love and support. My mom for being my editor/researcher/brainstormer. There would be no book without you.

Shawn Ott, for your help in making the hospital scenes and dialogue as realistic as possible.

Jenny Dean and Mary Speights, for lending me your expertise as English teachers and for doing the editing that I had begun to dread.

Kathy Cord, for your ability to take my sketches and jumbled ideas and turning them into an amazing painting (several of them, actually).

Darius Jones, for all the weekends I crashed at your place and bummed your food. Now you can officially tell everyone that this book was finished at your house.

And I would like to thank you, the reader. There would be no point in putting in the time and effort into this book if it weren't for you.

If you have any questions or comments, please feel free to email me at rick.loveday@gmail.com. You can also visit my Myspace page at www.myspace.com/rloveday. I'd love to hear from you.

www.ingramcontent.com/pod-product-compliance
Lightning Source LLC
Chambersburg PA
CBHW020831260626
47169CB00003B/930

Aztlánicon:

Conspiracy of the Senses